Oprah!
Before You Leave ...

Before I start
I bow ...
to the noble human race ...
because
the cosmic story tells
that "We, Humanity,"
we are all children of One God.

Elysse

WHO IS
ELYSSE POETIS?

I AM

I'm young,
I'm old,
I'm ICE!
I'm FIRE!
My wings are made of cosmic gold ...

Is this enough for your desire?

Your mysterious poetess, ELYSSE

COVERED IN FLOWERS

OPRAH! BEFORE YOU LEAVE ...

by Elysse Poetis™
AUTHOR/POET

EDITOR
Elizabeth A. Jordao

This first original published in 2010 by
VON DER ALPS PUBLISHING CORPORATION
www.vonderalps.com
CANADA

www.elyssepoetis.com

CANADIAN CATALOGUING IN PUBLICATION DATA

ISBN 978-0-9782302-7-2

Printed in U.S.A.

THE FUTURE IS OURS

To Oprah

her global guests and viewers

Thank You, ladies and gentlemen,
For your performances ...
For your genuine abilities to entertain ...
For delivering Oprah's talent and beautiful
shows to the interested viewers
via your kind participation.

Thank you, Oprah ...

HAPPY VIEWER
Canadian artist/author/poet/photographer
satirist—humorist

COVERED IN FLOWERS

Elysse Poetis and Marnie Richards, Exec. Dir. of BAC. Elysse received the Arts Acclaimed Award on May 1, 2008, at the Rose Theatre—The Performing Arts Centre in the City of Brampton, Ontario, Canada. Master of Ceremony, Anthony Sharewood, the famous Canadian producer/actor/director, who introduced Elysse and her book, The Mind of a Poetess.

The Future is Ours

Table of Contents

CONTENT: PAGE:

COVERED IN FLOWERS

CANADA

Photo © Elysse Poetis

The Queen Mother and Premier of Ontario, Hon. William G. Davis, legends who inspired me to live a life of honour. I received this original picture as a gift from a friend who knew how much I loved these two glorious lions. Look! God given grace, charm, elegance, intelligence—everything that true leaders display and we, the public, appreciate and admire.

Chapter One

THEATRICALLY YOURS

ELYSSE
ON
OPRAH

Fictively, I am going to be on Oprah. It happened unexpectedly in my mind. Soon after I arrived in Chicago, once again I realized the powerful energy that dominates the United States of America. These people are on the Moon! Actually I

COVERED IN FLOWERS

have the feeling that they are further, only we do not know, yet—since humanity stays safe if does not know everything that happen yesterday, in the present, or even 500 years ago. That's why some of us dream! We jump the fences of the conventional dimensions, see reality, then come back and write about it. That's how poets, musicians, scientists, and mostly parents, are able to use their gut feeling. Oh, ho, ho ... and there is more, but I'll live it alone. I have a farewell book to write based on my spontanious gut feeling. So, here I go!

Every time I cross the border from Canada I feel an overwhelming power in my surroundings—the soul of this phenomenal great country *The United States of America*. No wonder so many adventurers on Earth dream of coming to North America—US and Canada.

Like the US, Canada is similar in some

ways, and different in many other ways. While the US has this air of strength and the force of risk attached to its powerful spirit, Canada has enormous calm and discrete intelligence embedded in its glorious spirit. Canadians are so modest that someone like me (a daring promoter) could easily be mistaken for a US citizen. Well, I love the American spirit! I would have made a wonderful citizen myself if I would have chosen the USA from the refugee camp in Austria in 1980. But I chose Canada instead. I felt a deep attraction towards this gigantic beauty. Canada is under forty million people, one of the largest countries in the world— wealthy beyond imagination, and peaceful as a paradise. I love winters and forests! I love security and peace. I love the English language, French cooking and fashions ...

I love the Northern Lights ...

But now, fictively, I am in Chicago. With

COVERED IN FLOWERS

my super-sensibility I scan the surroundings and I find the seeds of progress pulverized over Chicago's entire map. From the quiet corner of my mind, I goggle its future ...

Suddenly, a close encounter of the minds—Me and Chicago:

"Good morning, Chicago! I'm here! I am Elysse! *The Love Promoter on Earth*. Today, fictively, I'll be on Oprah!"

Turning its face towards me, the city with the voice of a baritone answers:

"Good morning, Elysse! Welcome in my heart. From the luxurious four rooms in it, one is all yours tonight ... "

"Thank you, my dear Sir ... Chicago ..."

What a beautiful morning in front of the window—via memory savouring the city's history. Book after book, movie after movie, flowing through my mental river ...

THE FUTURE IS OURS

I smile ... Chicago, Chicago ... What a daring city. A beep on my phone alerts me that I shall head towards Harpo Studios.

I'm ready. The taxi takes me away. I'm closer and closer to Oprah, the greatest actress on television who intends to depart from her TV act.

On the way there I'm thinking and thinking—how like a giant Shirley Temple, full of giggles or facial expressions of fun and surprise, this actress, Oprah, successfully replaced *The Crosby's*—occasionally *The Golden Girls* and *Barbara Walters*. In fact, Oprah is not alone! Brilliance spreaded like wildfire in the last two decades. *Larry King, Anderson Cooper, Wolf Blitzer, Ellen, Judge Judy, Bones, CSI*(s)—along with me, have the globals mesmerized! Mary Hart from *Entertainment Tonight* is still a favourite. The ET excitement in the last decade successfully crossed the border where fresh blood was pumped into our Garden of Eden; youngsters, like the talented Ben Mulrouney. Then the elegant Catherine Clark on another favourite show of mine— the *CPAC (political)*. More *BBC*: Asia, Africa, Europe ... News and more news ... Science fiction vs reality ... UFO, USO and remote viewing phenomena unveiled; Gigantic talents hidden in modest skins; Oprah narrator for the *National Geographic;* Olympics, world soccer, hockey, American football, *Dancing With The Stars* ... I am forever intrigued! Politics and arts, my favourite mix, infinitely up-front ... Awards ... Fame ... Pain ... Love ... Drama ...

Oh, and there is more! A good example *The Discovery Channel*, with all its temptations—the universe expanding without our consent—galaxies in love ... in the mood for reproduction—Virgin Galactic travelling—flying cars ... On top of everything, I

THE FUTURE IS OURS

live in Waterloo Region, *The Technology Triangle of Canada*, where we feed daily on *Black Berries*. Research is in motion everywhere! Rejuvenation and longevity hidden in happiness. Human life span could drop the 'span' and replace it with the infinite. Oh, SIRT 1, the longevity gene, ready for activation, to give us immortality ... As a humorist I need strength, scientific nutrition and theoretic antioxidants to prevent mental stagnation. I know, I know!

Yes, I already divorced stress, and I marry love. *Polyphenols* and *Resveratrol* become also my targets. All of the above create comfort and happiness and—Love is it! *Love is the intelligence of intelligence*—yet, now knowing that I will live forever I developed the thirst for infinite knowledge.

Right now, Stephen Hawking's presence here is excellent for my super-microscopic vision of the future. I have the vission of

COVERED IN FLOWERS

The Future is Ours

one in 1.8 million I was told. My poetic dreams are in flower and will blossom even more as Her Majesty, Queen Elizabeth II and Prince Philip will arrive now on July 5th, 2010 ... I dream ...

Ladies and Gentlemen ... Forgive me ... I am Elysse Poetis, *The Hunter of Beauty*! In my creative momentum today, imaginary, I crossed the Canadian/US border in search of a new repertoire—the privilege to fictively be on the *Oprah Winfrey Show*. Oh, emotions ... poetic emotions ... The mental traffic congestion is holding me back. *But!*

I KNOW!

I'm used to risk!
I have tasted suspense!
I know the meaning of defense!
I live life's moments through impulse,
I know the rules!

Elysse

COVERED IN FLOWERS

Equipped with trust, I know I'll make it.

Ah, I did! I am inside the Harpo Studio. The security person was mesmerized by my wings of cosmic gold. From young to old, from ice to fire, I displayed my complete collection of Canadian flamboyant nordic charms.

Result?

Royal treatment, nothing less. You should see the orange armchair I am sitting on—it has space beyond my need. Embossed in its plush is a big O. Here, the discipline is as transcendent as the founder's spirit. It's Oprah's land in space—pure peace ...

Reception after reception, curious and investigative eyes are pinning me for telepathic contact. No one had ever encountered a a Canadian author like me; a global poetess, a love promoter on Earth, a hunter of beauty with wings of cosmic gold.

The Future is Ours

Through my cosmic age I carry the wisdom of time. Calmly, I surrender to everyone's curiousity—I let them visit my mind. Curious myself, I scan each character for my future art. I know I'll find stars! After all, *"I do believe that I do hold the pen of gold."* *"I'm in the world, yet not of it ..."* (continued in my art). Energetic, a producer makes her appearance, interrupting my peace ...

"Hello, Elysse. I'm Debra, one of Oprah's show producers."

"Hello, Debra, please to meet you."

"Elysse, we'll have a brief interview—I need to take some notes."

"Of course."

"My office is down the hall, we'll have to move there, please."

"Ok. Let's move."

Finally, I'm seated in Debra'd office. She's

calm and pleasant. I'm relaxed in her company. As she is preparing her recorder, I observe her. She's vibrant and all business. Cameras are everywhere. Composition is key. My moves are calculated, my breath, mathematical. I know how to be smart. After all, today I carry on my shoulders the reputation of my entire country. I am Canadian! Gifted with privileges and ingenuity beyond normality, and through cosmic times trained to act on any stage. Only God knows, I work hard for every moment of my existence. Here, while I familiarized myself with the surroundings, Debra prepared herself. Now she pulls her chair, seats carefully, and turns towards me smiling. With her delicate feminine finger presses the button on her recorder, *click!*:

D: "Elysse, what made you insist to be on Oprah's show?"

E: "Similarities in talent—from wanting

good on Earth to humour, plus the age, 56."

D: "You have an accent. What is it?"

E: "My two accents are Canadian and Romanian."

D: "You left Romania and Europe quite young. How young?"

E: "At 26, in 1980, I left Romania. At 27, in 1981, I left Europe."

D: "How hard was it to exit from behind the *iron curtains* and escape to Western Europe? How did you do it? How did you escape? Give me some details."

E: "To escape in 1980 was extremely difficult and dangerous. My life partner (my child's father) at the time was trained in special forces, so, we started preparing for our escape two years in advance, in 1978— finances, perfection, secrecy, code language, etc. We were together since I was seventeen (and he twenty-two). Two young souls so distant in spirit, yet so glued by fear and political circumstances—both unsure of what love was and consequently tortured minds.

Originally, in prior years, I did not think of any escape. First of all, I was very young. Secondly, when I heard how I have to escape, I was terrified! There was no easy solution. If he would have left without me, I would have been tortured and killed. If we left together and in the process I become a liability, I would have died anyway.

Miraculously, out of the blue, I received an official invitation from (then, West) Germany, from my childhood friend Katharina and her husband Werner. Back in Romania, like in a military plot, a legion of out of this world smart men prepared the perfect plan for my exit. To this day, I simply cannot believe it! Why did these people risk their lives for me? What did they see in me that they kept saying, *'You have to get out of here!'* These men felt that it was their God given mission to help me get out alive. To this day I'm asking myself, *'Why?'* Did they dream something? Did all of them have the same dream? Is this how God operates when *'it is to be?'*

Probably ...

So suffocating was my soul's atmosphere at the time, that from every breath I took I exhaled prayers—inhaling hope in return. The dangers and emotions are greatly expressed in my book, *The Mind of a Poetess.*"

D: "Elysse, I'll stop this preliminary testing here. By now I am convinced that you'll do fine in your interview with Oprah. Let me tell you that I also scrolled through your books on my Kindle last night, and I was impressed with your mind's stability. I wish you success in your conversation with Oprah, and thank you for your time."

E: "Thank you, Debra."

D: "Here, read our formal agreement and sign it for me, please."

E: "Let me grab my glasses. In fact, I do not need them for the small print even if it is only 4 point type. The smaller the print, the better I see it, providing it is a clean type face. Uh, this is easy. I'll read it fast."

D: "Elysse, feel free to touch up your makeup, or have a cup of tea ... water ..."

E: "Thank you. I will, Debra ... and here is the by-law, signed."

D: "Thank you. How refreshing to have to deal with someone from the industry. Apropos, the powder room is parallel. You still have half an hour to go."

The Future is Ours

E: "I'll admire the pictures on the corridor. I love pictures."

D: "Good. See you after the taping."

E: "See you."

With Debra gone, I started with the pictures on the walls. So many familiar faces, entertaining exhibitions, political figures, endeavours, and puppies, Oprah's favourite creatures, made of love.

The time has passed totally undetected. Some commotion forced me to focus on my surroundings. Suddenly, a slim petite lady approached me in a hurry.

"Here we go. Ready?" she asked.

"Yes!' I answered.

From the stage, Oprah's voice:

"Elysse! Come on out!"

E: "Yes, Oprah ..."

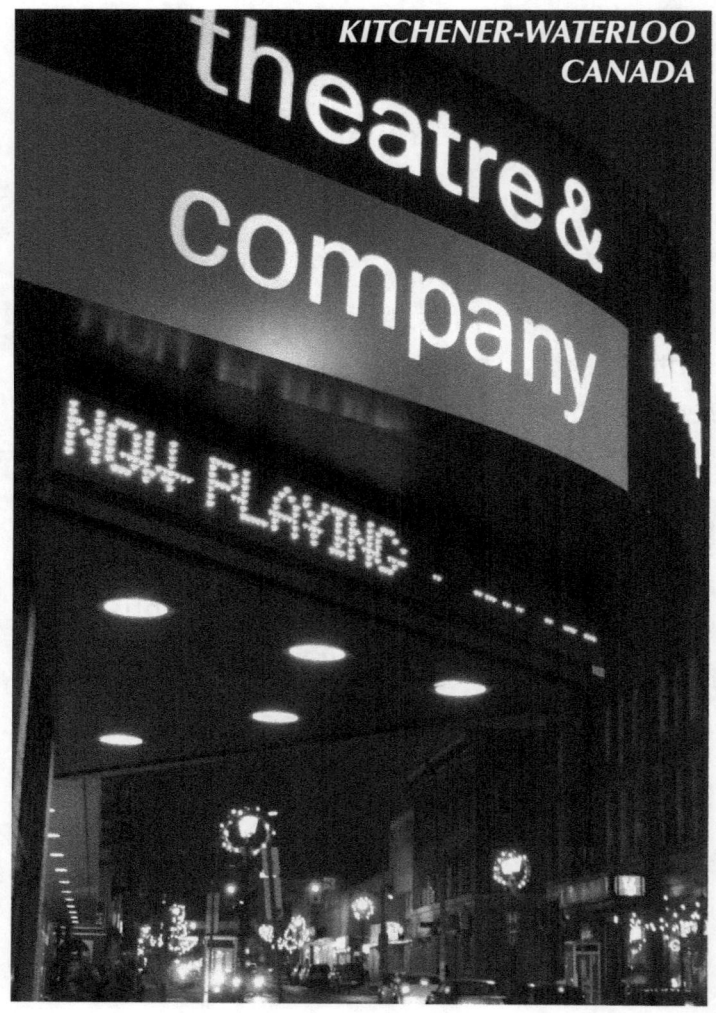

THE FUTURE IS OURS

O: "Let's see your face!"

E: "The face of the fifties ..." I laugh.

O: "Have a seat, Elysse. Welcome to Chicago! I heard a lot about you from my staff. You fascinated them! Now, down to reality—Let me tell you that over the years I've had many Canadians on my show, but none of them were born in Transylvania, the most famous gold mine of fiction. "

E: "The Author, Bram Stoker, really struck that golden cord with his entertaining imagination, didn't he?"

O: "Most certainly. Apropos, what is Transylvania like? From where all these fascination? Describe it—then, tell me about Canada and your impression of North America in general. I'm curious about your view. We have an hour—minus commercials, of course. I'll let you develop your answers. Give us details."

Covered in Flowers

E: "My pleasure. Detail is my forte. Let me start with Bistrita. I grew up in Transylvania near this city where the Irish/British author Bram Stoker started his original notes for what was to become the greatest fiction in English literature, *Dracula*. Approximately 280 movies were made based on Bram's fiction. To this day, Brad Pitt is exploring the depth of possibility of portraying Vlad, the prince, right there in Transylvania—guided by the real royals of today's Romania. Fascinating! Isn't it?"

O: "Get out of here ... I did not know that. Audience! Did you know than 280 movies were made based on one single book?"
Audience: Murmur ... "*No o o ...*"

"See? We did not know. Now I'm intrigued! Every time I think that I heard just about everything—boom! There comes the next shocker forcing me to accept the infinite possibility in it all."

THE FUTURE IS OURS

E: "Oprah, let me describe the land. Transylvania is beautiful. The air there is like mint. So fresh. So strong. Very healthy for the brain and the heart. The snow at the very top of the mountains does not melt easily. All around there are hills, valleys, forests, plantations, pastures ... Beautiful cities, with typical European architectures. Happy and hard working people, scholars, artists ... Clean markets, heavy with goods. Lots of very cute puppies ... This is not only what I remember from the first 26 years of my life living there, but something that I also experienced in 2007 during a brief visit there.

Now, the fascination with Transylvania?

I'm sure that transcends all the way back to the native Daciens and their kings. Even, later, Trajan Marcus Ulpius (Trajanus), the just and conscientious Roman Emperor who conquered Dacia in AD 101, and turned it into a province of the Roman Empire, must have been fascinated with this incredible place on Earth—for its strategic and demographic position in Europe. Look at the map from 10,000 years ago, and you will be surprised to see Romania's borders exactly as they are today. Only the name was changed by the Roman Empire, from Dacia to Romania. Even the Romanian language is perceived to be a romantic language of the world, and the closest descendant to the pure Latin language.

Everything that is important in the global education, previously was written in Latin: science, medicine, theology, philosophy, mathematics, law, poetry, etc. These days, Latin is totally embedded in the English language, an indispensable global commodity."

O: "It makes sense to consider the languages global assets. Without clean, clear language, there can never be global commerce, understanding, concession ..."

E: "In my opinion, communication is the solid gold of the 21st Century. It is your gift, my gift, and the gift of all those who pay attention to the global entrepreneurial spirit and fashion, and focus on education that matters. Good language is very important. Politically, language is very much like a mirror of a spirit of wisdom. Crucial!"

O: "You are committed to inspire. Keep talking, Elysse. I like it."

E: "My feeling is to totally trust that with the blossoming of so many new technologies, education will make a big jump within the next ten years, and we will see great improvement in communication, at the global level—consequently, in addition, improvement in the living standard/conditions. In fact, that's why I sent you my book in 2007—*The Mind of a Poetess,* which I

COVERED IN FLOWERS

Elysse with Prime Minister Bryan Mulroney, Legendary Premier of Ontario Bill Davis, Prime Minister Joe Clark, and Canada's Minister of Economy Tony Clement. (Millennium Dinner at Westin Castle, Toronto, and other political events).

wrote in 2001 while living a celibatic life in seclusion and going through a extremely difficult divorce. I wanted to share my enthusiasm—but ... you were so busy with the election."

O: "Right!"

E: "You worked for ... the left."

O: "Right!" (laughs) You're funny, Elysse."

E: "Only when I can mimic you."

O: "You mimic me?"

E: "And others. For example, when you narrate for the National Geographic—the way you say '*bug*'—I practiced that. Now, when I scroll the forests for tiny life to photograph, I ask Klaus, my husband, to let me know if there is any '*bug*' around."

O: "You did watch the program?"

E: "How can I miss it? I love watching documentaries and I care about bugs! I've been bugged all my life."

O: "You do love comedy?"

E: "Very much so."

O: "What type of comedy do you love?"

E: "Besides Mary Matalin and James Carville which I love watching and reading? Sincerely, British comedy would be my first choice. Then, to me, your show is often the best comedy—the girls of Madagascar ... The subjects you touch some times are so very entertaining, so refreshing. Of course, I do have a long list of favourites in the world of comedy which includes the parliaments around the world, and the royales."

O: "Do you watch comedy on television?"

E: "Everyone, dead or alive—television and movies. From *Dinner for One*, to *Bob Hope* at the White House or visiting the troops, to *The Crosby Show*, *Fresh Prince of*

The Future is Ours

Bel Air, Saturday Night Live, This Hour Has 22 Minutes, Royal Canadian Air Farce, Jim Carrey, Yuk-Yuk's, Rick Mercer, and the new comedians. Here in Canada some of them are just super-talented artists. I even watch German comedy. They have some phenomenal shows! *Everybody Loves Raymond* and *The Golden Girls*, I watched with equal pleasure as I would watch *Keeping up With Appearances*. Then, *Mr. Bean* in his comic rituals and glory. What a talent!

What shocks me is the fact that some of the best comedians do not get paid what they deserve. Like in art, often the not so good ones get paid in millions for their work, while the very talented struggle. It is the same with authors. Probably the best examples we can look at are those that received famous awards for literature and poetry that they did not create at all. Many just collect poetry, assemble some pages, enter competitions, and it is all legal. What is even more disturbing is the fact that they end up being called poets and authors, when in reality they are just collectors and sellers of other people's work.

O: "You'll take care of that discrepancy, I sense. By using humour you can actually do a lot of good. Stay calm and do it. That's how I operate. I think it—I plan it—I do it."

E: "I'm equipped and prepared mentally not only to entertain the planet from every corner, but to save it all. Along my greatest efforts will be encouraging people to use art to express themselves. Write, paint, sing, dance, teach. And, yes, I trust that artists will be paid in the future—not only attention, but an income. All artists in the world need to continue to create without major agonies leading to fatigue, and consequently forcing them to give up on art. Arts are needed to beautify our minds, our homes, our cities, our countries, our lives. Our planet needs beautification!"

O: "You are all over the map, Elysse. I can sense your satellite scanning all life and events on Earth. Clearly you want to see a stronger, smarter future for humanity and there isn't any television show that could give you the space or the time to fully expose your abilities, to express your love for humanity, or your trust in the brilliance of the future. Internet is becoming that channel for all of us."

E: "Thank God for the communication channels. Thank God for those individuals who drive the industry, invest in it. You're one of them, Oprah. I can't wait to see the future with your cable network and young blood creatively pumped to maintain it."

O: "You are well informed, Elysse. Do you watch the news continuously?"

Covered in Flowers

E: "With conviction. I watch and read everything. I am a sponge of information."

O: "Beside our age we do have many things in common. Through history, every corner of this Earth has been touched by both good and evil, and it is up to us to continue to carry the negative or the positive memories on board. Let me give you the freedom to use the next few minutes and compact your view of the world—past, present, future. What do you want the millions of viewers around the world to discover from your mind today?"

E: "First, I'd love to let humanity know that *The Future is Ours—Covered in Flowers*. I'd also like them to know that I was created to be a writer for a good reason, and I believe that the written word is a very powerful tool that can reach every corner of our planet, inspiring generations to come. Nothing can stop me from feeling the way I feel about the capabilities of our human race and the extraordinary future that is knocking daily at our global door.

My books are written in the most prosperous and wealthiest country in the world, where people are strong, smart and kind. Canada has shaped me into a fine global. Canadians share their God given resources with the entire world—just as I share my mind through my books, encouraging and invigorating the human race. Through my stories and poetry I also fight the war against the insufferable evil which in rotation operates through humanity, putting us against each other, suggesting limitation on the horizon and apocalyptic misery.

Well, I disagree with nayers! Humanity is young in cosmic age. We are babies in the universe! We are just starting out. Love for beauty is what we need! The future is the greatest beauty awaiting for us—all we

COVERED IN FLOWERS

TORONTO

THE FUTURE IS OURS

have to do is to believe and start walking towards it. Just as a baby takes his/her first steps towards the mother or the father, and in the process takes some falls, that's how we are. But soon, we will learn to walk towards the future. Even if we fall at times, we will stand up and try again. Imagine God proud of us when we'll be able to make it across the spectrum of life.

Love and respect for each other and for all creation are the weapons that can chase the nonsense away. Let's use them, globally! We need to respect the past, present, and the future. These times were, are, and will be our lessons needed to upgrade our wisdom—preparing us for our next cosmic step ... and the next ... and the next ...

We have to be clean, smart, focussed, organized, and believers in the possibility of higher cosmic times. Hope springs out of that daring vision that there is a very fine future awaiting for us. All children of the world need hope through encouragement—which means much more than anything else. Spiritual food means smart teachings.

You and I, Oprah, did not have much right after the second war when we where born. Did we? Often we went to bed with very little in our stomachs, yet we were happy because, thank God, we had positive people around us—at least half of them were positive. In my case, what kind of stories do you think I heard from both sides?

The positive people were pointing to the future, while the negative people were pointing at the half exposed corpses of all those German children/boys killed all over the place, boys who were ripped out of their safe family environments and sent to war against war veterans who killed them like insects. Our parents witnessed it all.

THE FUTURE IS OURS

Oh, and all those young German girls taken to Siberia ... raped, killed, destroyed for life ... Young German mothers were also taken to Siberia in labour camps. Left behind were the babies and small children. The teenagers were killed in the war.

Imagine the hearts of these young mothers, not knowing anything about the children. Many families, Romanian, Hungarian, Slavic, and Romms (Gypsies), took these children under their wings and delivered them back to the mothers when (or if) they came back from Siberia.

Some of these young mothers came back pregnant or with more children, products of rape. Even so, the human heart is infinitely loving. All these children were protected from the cruel reality of their provenance. Secrecy was needed and the communities agree on codes of conduct. No one ever insulted the children. The fathers who vanished during the war were one set, but there were the ones who left their families behind and headed for the Western World without a trace. Orphans were everywhere! Some mothers never returned from Siberia, and the fathers disappeared also.

Oh, the trauma. These Germans were there for thousands of years! They built the most impressive seven cities in Transylvania. It was their home! The same with Hungarian people born in Transylvania for generations. Recall that Transylvania was also for a while under the Austro-Hungarian Empire crown? As we can only imagine, all nationalities suffered immensely. Only later they started to enjoy education in their own languages, including high school and university level.

Speaking of suffering during and after the greatest wars, the Romanian people were flipped like a pancake, with a spatula, from one side to another—and there was nothing they could do. A small country of decent people who never attacked or attempted to conquer anyone. During *The Second World War* Romania was flipped really good in terms of dominance: from one extreme to another—from nazi (extreme socialism) to stalinism (extreme communism).

Year 1953: Stalin died in April; 25 year-old Queen Elizabeth II took her Coronation oath on June 2; On August 8, I was born.

As you can imagine, the stories were very fresh. In the future I'd greatly appreciate some clear movies/documentaries reflecting those times. I'm still curious. I'd love to see documentaries from the European perspective. Considering how I was pounded with so much information as a young child, it is interesting to me the fact that I never felled the need to argue or agonize over the events—but I was very curious about the

45

entire thing, mainly the clear reasons—economical, political, etc. As children and students in totalitarian communism, there was nothing I could do to explore facts. The communist teachings had brushed aside everything that posed a treat to their image—mainly the truth.

Apart from schools, children were feed stories and images from all around about the general fever in Europe, and around the world. It is unbelievable! Isn't it? What mainly fascinates me is the *brother against brother*, the family war, so speaking of the Anglo-Saxon race, fighting each other for clarity and dominance.

Hmm ... Complexity vs complexity. Infinite stories were circulating about how many Jewish children were hidden and protected by the good people of Romania—every nationality living there. (Forget the few extremists—every country has them).

THE FUTURE IS OURS

One of my greatest mentors and protectors escaped death, while his mother, father, two sisters, and a brother were taken away forever. He was 13 years old when he chose to jump off the train that was heading for Auschwitz. It was three o'clock in the morning when he took that risk and jumped in a revive, and survived. A Hungarian family took him in, changed his name immediately, and protected him from harm.

He turned into a fine young man, becoming Romania's champion in boxing (heavyweight category). He studied classical music, became a music professor, then went higher and higher in progress. Later, he fell in love with the daughter of that couple who saved him, got married and had a beautiful baby girl, Yolanda.

Time passed and the young man become a tenor, performing on famous stages in Cluj/Klausenburg, Budapest, and in Vienna.

COVERED IN FLOWERS

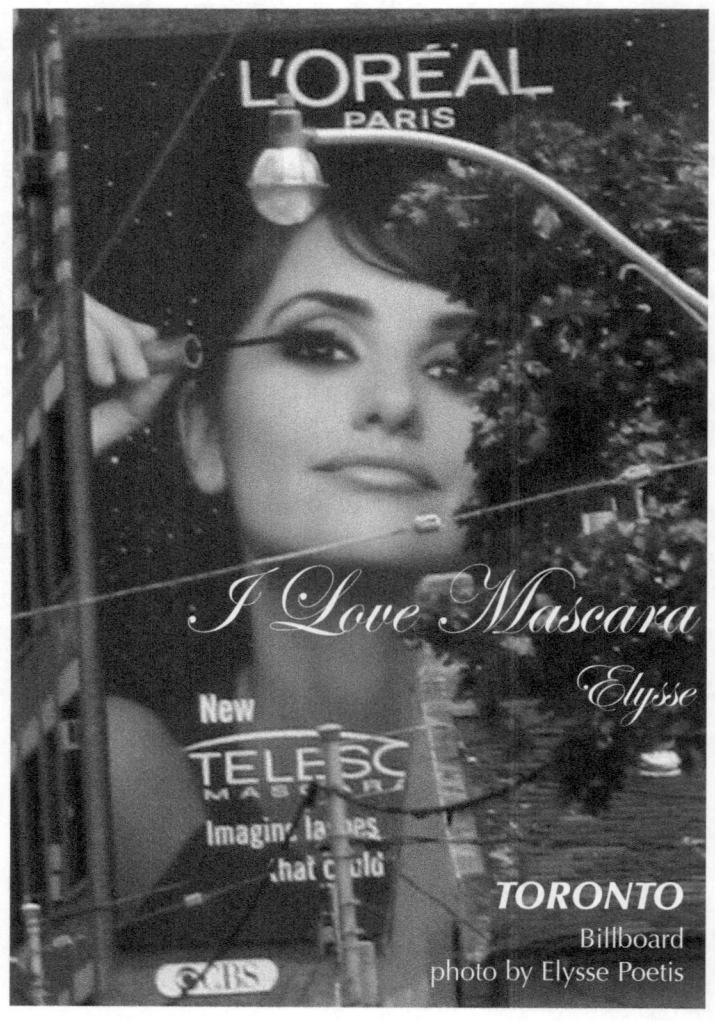

The Future is Ours

Yolanda was a teenager when her parents, sadly, decided to divorce. Two years down the road, her father introduced her to his fiance, a very elegant lady, Elena.

How do I know his story so well?

Let me describe briefly how it happened, and what a lucky girl I was to have the privilege to meet this honourable spirit in this life: It was 1976, summer time, on a warm, crisp sunny day in the city Arad, Romania. I heard from a friend, an economist who now lives in New Zealand, that The School of Arts had a few spots to fill and the competition is strong. Believing in impossible was embedded in my attitude, so I quietly started planning how I should be one of the lucky future students of that famous art school. I wasn't going to let that to chance, so, I prepared my approach. Not knowing anything about the location, school CEO/director, size, number of students, etc., my thinking was that of a child. After I found the necessary leads, I dressed elegantly, went to the head office which was in a palace like building, and once there, I almost panicked. The glory of those stairs ... Shivers went down my spine. Just a few years prior I lived in a small community where no such things existed. Oh, how emotional I got at the bottom of those stairs ... and how I started praying to God for a miracle ...

Was I naive? Now, as I look back, I think that it was brilliant the way I attracted my destiny in that instance. Believe me, it may sound childish or naive, but it was not. Look how I prayed and what happened. I prayed to God that a gigantic spirit incorporated in a powerful presentable man is the CEO/director; that he would come out from behind those gigantic elegant french doors and see me; he would come towards me, take my hand and be my instant friend; that I'll know instantly that I passed the exam, and this powerful man will remain my mentor and protector through all my years there until I graduate. Oh, God, I'll make him proud ... I'll respect him. I'll love him for loving me ...

With my eyes on that prominent door at the central top of the stairs, holding on to the stairs' banister, I was in a trance, when all of a sudden light come out of that very room. Stunned, I nearly paralyzed. First, a shadow on the door ... then the most presentable giant man I have ever seen ... white wavy hair, broad shoulders, masculine face, sublime smile ... and he was coming down the stairs towards me. My big eyes were wide open, absorbing the sketch of my very prayer coming down the stairs. Involuntarily, I brightened up ... releasing my sweet natural smile, almost like I had just rejoined in a long lost friendship.

He was tall in his elegant custom made black suit, silk tie patterning violins, bright white shirt—sleeves secured with elegant golden buttons, and a pair of beautiful green eyes to forever remember. He stopped on the last step above me, then slowly stepped down in front of me—towering over my young feminine fragility and my huge hazel eyes sparkling on fire. Quiet and smiling, he stretched his arm inviting my hand in his hand. As his quiet lips pressed a kiss on my hand, I lost all my senses. I was floating ... What seemed as an eternity turned into step-repeated eternities due to his silence—preserving the emotional trance. Finally, a lift of an eyebrow and the sound of a masculine voive of an angel coming out of him:

"Hello," he said as he bowed gently to me. "I am Zahu Ioan, and you are? ..."

THE FUTURE IS OURS

"Elysse ... Elysse ... Maria."

"Maria ... come with me Maria," he said while taking my hand and guiding me up the stairs towards the very door that gave me those incredible emotions while I was praying. Again, not a word was spoken. We arrived in front of the french door with him angelically holding my hand like a prince in fairy tales. With his left hand he opened it, led me in, and slowly shut it behind us. The room was immense. Tall windows, classy furniture, books well organized, a reception area, and at our right—a grand piano ...

"Maria," he almost whispered. "Let me sing to you." He placed his hands on my waist and lifted me like I was a feather, placing me right on top of the piano. Oh ... what that did to my heart. Suddenly, heavenly notes climbing up my spirit, escorted by the voice of an angel:

Covered in Flowers

"Ave Maria ... Ave Maria ..."

For a moment I thought that I died and went to heavens. Sitting there at his left, he would look up at me from time to time, continuing to mesmerize my spirit with his charms and the variety of vocal tones—soft and powerful. If someone would have injected me with a needle, I don't think I would have felt it. I was floating.

Now, this was a moment I will never forget! I'm very much aware today that these things do not happen to everyone. Must be very rare. Looking back I have to thank God for the numerous fun and beautiful moments I was blessed with. Treasurer's of this sort are extremely empowering to all of us. We need this! We need miracles! ... or make belief miracles. The rest of the story I'll have to write in detail at some point, sometime in the future. My entire life in Romania was an out of this world miracle.

THE FUTURE IS OURS

Brief conclusion? Mr. Zahu Ioan became one of my most honourable mentors and a trusting friend. At that particular time, as you can only imagine, I knew before the exam that I passed—mainly because he tested my artistic talent that very first day. I was very good at art. Here, in Canada, I sketched patterns for Vogue, for Disney, and an enormous numbers of industries—everything from packaging design, to fabrics, wallpaper, ceramics, etc.

In publishing, as an artist and art director, I also used my talents to make all those business magazines look good. I love beauty. I like seeing it displayed and I work hard to push it up front. Beauty needs visibility! Beauty is love. We all have beauty within ourselves. Let's use it as a tool to help guide the next generations in the right direction.

Canada has delivered incredible talent! We work hard here and take art seriously.

COVERED IN FLOWERS

Walking in the book stores and detecting my face between the stars of the world, in the beginning it shocked me. Then, I started thinking—That's where I belong! I am Elysse.

THE FUTURE IS OURS

Many of Disney's top illustrators are graduates of Sheridan College. So is one of my best friends, Sonya G. Peters, who became one of Australia's most prominent artists. In fact she achieved greatness overall, and she is also lecturing art at university on the Gold Coast. Our beautiful Sonya is Australian now. I can tell you that she always was ahead of her times, protecting and promoting the beautiful environment and children. Her art reflects her passion and it is highly appreciated. I love Sonya.

Going back to our previous discussion, wars are terrible tools of change. Like volcanos—mixing the earth. Wars have the property to mix the human race, but also to hurt everyone. Everyone's tears are painful. Death is not pretty for anyone. People who are carriers of love energies suffer even at the sight of the news. Myself, I can not count how many times I cried in front of the television set. Through history, those who could tell the stories and show the pictures were few. Thank God for the printing press, the smart communicators, and those photographers and film makers who risked their lives bringing us the images of 'some' truth.

On behalf of all the Europeans and the North Americans who died during *The First and The Second World Wars*, the biggest in the world ever, I'll have to be able to recognize that they did not die in vain. Tens of millions of Europeans, scattered all over Europe, involved or in the way—I think of them, I write about them, I even dream of them.

Not once did I imagine that a high resolution picture taken via satellite could show accurately the human remains. A computer able to read from above the DNA splattered all over at that time, could put to rest the argument of who suffered most. Everyone

THE FUTURE IS OURS

involved suffered loss and pain even after these great wars expired. Few family members who returned from these wars remained strong. The majority died of injuries, depression, diseases, or suicide.

In those days, you could not see handicapped people. They were isolated from the society. Artificial arms and legs were a rarity. We, the baby boomers, born right after to compensate for the large number of humans that died prematurely, we suffered, too. Malnutrition was common. Until my adulthood, I myself was an anemic, on the verge of getting leukemia. Mines were all over. Distrust carried on for a while.

But people changed all that! They stopped talking about the war and hardship, and started building a new attitude. They concentrated on education, prosperity, and a bit of fun. Of course it was the Elvis Presley era and the Beatles. Education, elegance, good language, romance, dance, a bit of wine with cheese ...

Wars are like bees. They carry the pollen of DNA from one country to another. Even the soldiers dying today, we bring their bodies home, yet there is plenty of their blood spilled all over, absorbed in the Earth beneath. That blood is forever alive right there where is spilled. That's why I think that we should fly over the planet and bless it all. Pulverize it not only with tears of love and holy water, but seeds of wild flowers to make them grow everywhere. Look at the banners in this book: *The future is ours— Covered in flowers*. What if all the people that died were all of us? ... now re-incorporated, heaving our second chance ...

Here, in Waterloo, science is the powerhouse. I did mention that Stephen Hawking is here right now, and Her Majesty, Queen Elizabeth II, has just arrived in Canada, and

The Future is Ours

is heading for Waterloo soon. I heard in the news that she will visit RIM Corporation. RIM is (means) *Research In Motion*, the progressive and impressive giant that gave birth to *Black Berry*. If you have a Black Berry, remember, it comes from right here, my neighborhood, minutes from where I write.

Oh, let me tell you what I heard on TV from a gentleman who wrote a book about RIM and its founder(s). Just listen to this: RIM set up a modern building where top of the line scientists indulge in *'out of this world thinking'* while playing golf, relaxing, indulging in a type of entertainment that would make a French royal elite look pale. Now, here is the yummy part! The reason for such extravagant treatment of these scientists is to give them space, time and opportunity to blossom in ideas. Waterloo could give birth to the next Einstein!

Isn't that magnificus ... (great in deeds).

Above, Research In Motion, RIM, where your precious Black Berries are being born—where the future is present.
Below, at Wilfrid Laurier University, Waterloo, students from around the world are indulging in advanced 21 Century studies.

THE FUTURE IS OURS

My suggestion? Smart people of the world! It's time you pack your bags and move here with your protégé children. Young ones, come to universities here! Who knows? What if it's you? Or your child? ... to help us follow the cosmic beep.

See how easily I derouted you from the war? It works—does it not? We need beautiful stories. Promising ones. RIM like corporations that invest in brilliance. Famous scientist and royalty. We love it all! Please, my friends, in your minds choose progress because we need to jump the cosmic fence to the next level, another pyramid.

Yes, you can, and you are free to do so. Let's not forget that the individual makes the country, the individual makes the peace. And yes, the society needs protection from individuals who are strongly attracted to argument, deceit, corruption— inexplicable silly evil, so speaking.

COVERED IN FLOWERS

Evil Does Exist—is the title of one of my poems. But, we can fix the evil by showing its followers *'reality from above'*—help them realize the nonsense of stagnation vs the future. No followers—no power, right?

Apropos: When I say, *'Yes, you can,'* I did not mimic President Obama. I wrote that in 2001 (pg. 179) and I publish it in 2006, far before President Obama used it. Language is for all of us to share, and yes, we overlap our ideas many times. That's why I wrote *Collision of Ideas* right at the beginning of that book. I believe that it is beautiful, and we can do everything together, much better. All we have to do is *'do it!'* The CEO of gigantic Random House would agree. He said that, too. Going back to the story, tell me my friends, how many times have we asked ourselves, "Can we have a world without war?"

Answer? Of course, we can!

THE FUTURE IS OURS

How? How can we eliminate at once the multitude of wars going on all over the planet at any given time? *"One God—One throne, to set the tone for the entire human race—That's what we miss!"* (another quote from my book).

Through my entire opera I exposed both sides. Rational thinking and acting it seams to me springs out of suffering. The more we suffer, the smarter we become. The day we surrender in our minds to the idea that our business is to be the best that we can be every single day—to cry out loud if life hurts—then to sober up—shake it off—and think and act within reason, that, my friends, is a sign that wisdom has arrived. We are home in our minds! ... and comfortable.

Another question, "Do we need to strike the evil?" As a global society we have the responsibility to keep our smart environment safe. That's why we have state versus small lawless tribes as once our ancestors had (very few, to this day, preserve such fashions).

These days, being a global family made up of billions of us, we treasure: love, prosperity, peace, travelling, commerce, education, and smart politics—we look forward towards a complimentary future. Imagine how good we are going to look to other cosmic nations ... *Civilized Planet Earth* beautiful and smart, out of ashes! ... now pure gold.

My friends, we need to believe! We need to dream! Here, in Canada, baby boomers are enrolling in universities in great numbers. They all believe!

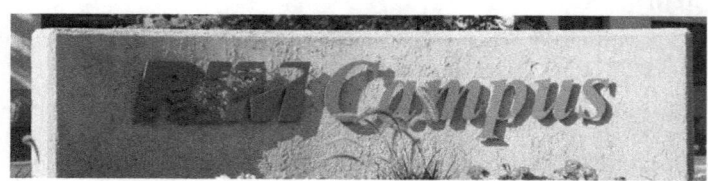

SENSIBILITY IS A QUALITY, UP TO A POINT

Sensibility is a quality, up to a point!
Sensibility prolonged and/or taken to extremes
can become a liability! A nightmare!
To any: person, nation, planet, galaxy, universe.

Complaints stretched over thousands of years can
make us look ...
How?

Here, I don't have to mention other parts of the
world, just the world I come from and the world I
belong to—Europe and North America.
These two continents carried the two greatest
wars in the history of humanity.
Even seniors, women, children,
horses, dogs and pigeons, fought!
... during ... and after ... millions died ...

Europe was flat on its face!
Every country involved was damaged, hurt,
hungry, angry and insulted to the limits.

COVERED IN FLOWERS

By whom?

By their own GOD given destinies,
destinies that in the end made them
the greatest on Earth!

In war, good or bad, all people suffered!
(Including the dictators).

Yet, these continents picked up the pieces
and rose above the past glorious, civilized,
educated, fashionable, lovable and kind enough
to share their spiritual resources (strength)
and economic success (knowledge)
with the rest of the world.

Now, that's what I call a healthy attitude!

Perfection?

Probably never.
Continuous love, kindness,
prosperity and beauty?
Always, forever.

THE FUTURE IS OURS

See, my Global Friends, how GOD placed me right at the heart of
of this radical game? "Communism vs Democracy?"
I don't gamble, my friends. I love DEMOCRACY.
ELYSSE

***

Dear Oprah, since you gave me the green lights to say it all, or as much as I can imaginary compact in 200 pages, or so—I'd like to say thank you, to you, and all other talented people in the entertainment business who made me laugh, even when I did not have anyone to laugh with. Perfect example of loyalty to happiness is our very Betty White. What a perfect mirror of a living legend. Right now, she's energizing us all! I will forever treasure the day I paraded in front of the studio where *The Golden Girls* was filmed, at MGM Studios, Disney. With regret, I faced the sad news of losing one actress after another.

Finally, Oprah, I'd like to invite my *Global*

COVERED IN FLOWERS

Friends to read my books. My books and my writing talent is similar to Michael Jackson's musical and dancing talent. My heart is also the same. I believe in Black and White, and all other colours in the spectrum of existence. Apropos, Michael's Black & White is my favourite—and him writing poems up in the tree is also pleasantly embedded in my memory.

In his art, Michael targeted the Moon. In my art I target the Sun. After a few years of writing I realized my inclination. In Michael's art, people were moved by the rhythm. In my art people are responding to the rime. Michael fell love when on stage. I feel love when I write. In *The Mind of a Poetess* I describe in great detail the agony of being out of the trance.

Oprah, I do believe that everyone who is creative, regardless of the field, feels pain and love. That's why excellence comes out

The Future is Ours

of them. If we look carefully around the world we will see the labour of love, the mark of so many humans who sadly never made it in any news. *'Every nation has its best—Search for them, please do not rest,'* I suggest in my writings.

- Music and poetry—forever in love.

- Architecture and glory—reflection of power.

- Civilization in nations—spiritual grace.

- A planet of peace—the best living place.

And so on ... I believe ... and I write ...

The art of comedy is also healthy for the soul. Many, who already started reading my books, tell me how much they see themselves in my art. Many cry and laugh while reading. If they feel down, betrayed, lost, insulted, suicidal—or if they are struggling with love or loss, my books give them strength and hope, calms their spirits. Those who dream beyond reality also find my books extremely informative, empowering and delightful. Many become committed in their search for love. Somehow, in my writings I managed to simplify everything a human needs answers to. There is no corner of life untouched—no stone unturned. There is truth about everything for everyone.

When I was young, my curiousity got me in trouble many times, especially with my mother who always was a very conservative Baptist. She believes in a way in which made me very uncomfortable as a young child. Not once did I confront her ideologies, only to find myself punished for defending the cave people who never heard of the Bible. "Why should someone who never learned how to read, or heard of this or that doctrine, go to hell?"—was my question. My mother did not have an answer for me, and the shortest way to a christian gold medal for her, was to punish me.

There is a lot of deceit and immorality which needs fixing not only in the world of religions, but in the world overall.

Can we do it?

Yes! Education will take us there, one step at a time—and I mean more common sense education that just fancy conversations (that too, it's fun). Through the channels of communication by speaking a common global language, expressing the desire to be a global family, *one for all—and all for one*, we can achieve peace and understanding. Less silly theatrics and more action could speed the process of progress—or at list the acceptance that progress is here and all we have to do is, embrace it.

Can we do that?

Fairy tales are suppose to be elegant and

rewarding. Our globe and all of us deserve a gigantic fairy tale.

Galactically, we are in for enormous surprises—and there is more! The universal celebration, between all galaxies and universes. Imagine that! We, "*At The Galactic Table*," is in my book. So is "*God's Visit to Earth, I & II*," just ask Larry King and Dolly Parton. They were there! At nine o'clock sharp God knocked on the CNN's door. Like Moses, Dolly ended up reading the holy plaques. Former President Bill Clinton was there, too, playing the sax. Her Majesty, the famous queen, delivered the welcome speech. The first twins asked God what brand of perfume is that on Him?

Oh, let me give you a tiny piece of my poem, GOD'S VISIT TO EARTH II—without the beginning or the end in it. Even Larry King could enjoy it. "Larry, I watched you. I love you. Happy future! Have fun." Enjoy ...

GOD'S VISIT TO EARTH

II

I could find a splendid flute,
A little John to pay salute,
A Chelsea with her hair in waves
Could impress and could amaze!
The King of Skies,
I dream ...

Bill himself could play the Sax!
Celine Dion could sing for Him!
Embraced with every magic dream
Globals could happily dance,
I dream ...

Prince William could shake His hand!
The First Twins could ask,
What brand of perfume is that? ... on Him ...
I dream ...

Her Majesty, the famous queen,
Dressed vivid for The Supreme,
Could deliver the welcome speech ...

75

COVERED IN FLOWERS

The globe could be host to angels,
Without worries of the dangers!
Just elegance ... peace ... and dream ...
Embraced by a future well deserved,
Under the universal kingship of The Sublime ...
I dream ...

That day,
The Honorable GOD of Peace
Could deliver every piece,
Every cosmic puzzle!
Of course, the ones we miss.

In the effort of growing smart,
We need to dream!
Don't we?

I dare to imagine theatrically a day
When all the smart that walk the Earth
Will invite GOD to their lands
Showing Him the place of birth
From where the strongest human minds
Grew with cosmic thirst,
I dream ...

76

THE FUTURE IS OURS

But now, just imagine ... On Larry King
At nine o'clock, suddenly! ... a magic knock ...
GOD interrupting his show,
As He does, as we all know,
When He wants to intervene.
Look!
The cover of *TIME Magazine*
profiling the divine image!
Right there, Dolly, with her cleavage,
Holding a plaque in her hand, declares,
Wow! And here is a new commandment!
Folks! We need global agreement.
Imagine that!
My Global Friends ...

The day humanity will adopt peace,
GOD could be pleased ...
The children happy ...
Seniors smiling ...
Kings complying ...
The youth dancing ...
The responsible adults processing
The dream ...

continued in *The Mind of a Poetess* *ELYSSE*

My friends, you all have the Ice and Fire within yourselves. Stand up and go resolve your lives! Yes, you can. You can even help others. Through life, always, please consider failure and injustice just a lesson. We all do mistakes every day, but that does not mean that we should stop trying again. We have to go on, and we can.

LOVE IS

Love is the highest form of Cosmic Intelligence,
The most painful beauty of all existence,
The most mysterious truth of life.

To love we must. ELYSSE

Poems and text above writen in 2001
on pages 30-31-32 and 179—continued in *The Mind of a Poetess*

***

O: "Elysse, you are history on wills. I think I needed this experience, I mean to imaginary seat down with a 29 year old Canadian who 26 years prior was born in communist

The Future is Ours

Romania—lived in famous Germany and Austria for 1 year, making her a 56 years old baby boomer gifted with the talent of writing and debating life from every corner.

You see, Elysse, I never lived in communism, and the greatest world wars, overall, did not take place over my skies. I believe that all valuable lessons are embedded in history. You managed to make me curious. I want to know more. Starting next year, I'll have plenty of time on hand. You keep writing, my girl. I'll keep you in mind."

E: "For me, reading is daily fun, Oprah. Why don't we take our fishing ropes right now, and head for the banks of *Amazon*. The variety of books that we can target ... There is also a new species, a unique modern electronic reading device called *Kindle*—the caviar of all. May I ask why *O Magazine* is not yet on Kindle? Every book of mine is on Kindle. Convenient prices, too. I love Kindle! The planet loves Kindle.

O: "Elysse, this year is a very busy one for me. Will I survive the pressure? I think about my well being every morning before I start. Calm in solid in my mind, yet the numerous events on my calendar feel like cold showers in middle of the night. Fishing for knowledge on Amazon sounds tempting and I greatly appreciate your invitation, but it will be next year. O Magazine has to go on Kindle also, I agree. I'll get to that."

E: "Oprah, Oprah, about your departure ... it is great discomfort. In the beginning, like Medusa, you lured us nicely into your cave, impregnated our minds with your ideas of fun—and now, abandoned us on the global streets of communication to find someone else to give us a ride home. It is not easy to become addicted to a face, a voice or fun of a special sort, then wipe it out of your mind, just like that.

The Future is Ours

Do you see what you did to us? Exactly when we managed to create permanent space in our calendars for your show, convince our spouses, children, friends, and neighbours that you are the one to be watched—Boom! You slapped us with the news of separation—and no chance for reconciliation.

Does it work? Am I funny enough? My Siamese cat, Mitzy, just said, *'meow'*—meaning, yes. Oh, Oprah ... This is not funny. All this time on hand without you. Hmm ... I like what you did to us! You chose this smart business that made you wealthy. We chose to watch you to help you get wealthy, then listen to you telling us how ... What was it that you told us?

Pardon me ... I already forgot! I just realized that, like you, I can be a very busy baby boomer. I am a daughter to an 83 year old mother who by now seriously needs my

COVERED IN FLOWERS

Above, my husband Klaus. Speaking of the power of attraction—I prayed for a brave King of Northern Lights, a lion capable to love, like the one on the left—and I received exactly what I prayed for. The blue eye and the sword were included.

This doll was my model for the man of my dreams.

assistance. A wife to a gentleman who deserves tons of attention and love. A mother to a young lady who is just discovering life. A grandmother to some of the most adorable babies. I'm pleasantly busy!"

O: "You are funny. Keep talking. Say anything you want as long as you want. Give this imaginary show a record longevity. Come on, Elysse! Go, go. Talk."

E: "Thank you, Oprah. I really thank you for abandoning us. Now, along with my fellow Canadians, former viewers of yours, I'll watch again and faithfully *One on One* with Peter Mansbridge from our CBC, (*Canadian Broadcasting Corporation*). He is the most watched in Canada. I hope he is not retiring considering that right now his book is a bestseller, not to mention that he lives in Stratford—the home town of Justin Bieber, minutes from me. This tiny town, Stratford, is a Shakespearean stage from one end to another. Actors, including Peter's beautiful lady, are acting everywhere, even on the terraces of their own homes. Oh, the language—*British at its best*. Oprah, movies can not deliver what reality does.

Christopher Plummer, the charming Canadian actor and main character along Julie Andrews in *The Sound of Music*, (the Von Der Trapp family)—this gentleman is a regular in Stratford Festivals, performing in a miraculous Shakespearean fashion, acting for which I would have given him multiple global awards if I had the power. This phenomenal artist lives a life of dedication to quality on stage—assorté, those glamorous looks and the talent of a giant. I always loved Mr. Plummer."

O: "Sorry to interrupt, Elysse, but I just brewed the idea of coming to Stratford with my musical. In 2011 I'll have the time."

THE FUTURE IS OURS

E: "That's a brilliant idea! Please, come. Two years ago I spotted your poster in the elevator at the Rose Theatre in Brampton, of course, beside the bill-boards in Toronto."

O: "You pay attention to my art ... You have my attention in exchange."

E: "Thank you. It's true. Everything positive in nature attracts me and provokes me to promote: people, products, events, etc."

O: "Since we get along so well, let me give you space to just play, ask random questions. Tell random stories."

E: "Brilliant! I waited for this! Here comes my question: Did you ever asked yourself who, beside you, in our history would have been wildly watched on television? I can tell you right now that I did! I thought of it, and two people come to my mind: Princess Diana and former President Bill Clinton."

Covered in Flowers

O: "Together?"

E: "Duo or solo."

O: "Now that you said it, I think that it is true. Their charm and charisma would have attracted mega numbers as viewers."

E: "Three years ago, I went with my husband to see former President Bill Clinton in Hamilton. Wow! The positive, enthusiastic crowd there, present just like us for the very reason not to miss the chance in this lifetime. This man has heavenly charms! Even he must be shocked at the love and respect directed at him."

O: "It's true. Now let me ask you, does Canada have charming leaders?"

E: "In Canada, Prime Minister Piere Trudeau was a great charmer. Right now, Prime Minister Stephen Harper is a young charming, vibrant leader, very talented and sharp in policies—also an extraordinary communicator in both English and French. He resembles JFK a bit."

O: "True again. Any others?"

E: "Many. Past and present. Here just an example: Former Premier of Ontario, Hon. Bill Davis, to this day is being perceived as Canadian royalty. Some time ago, our former Prime Minister Brian Mulroney had a book signing event at the Bay and Bloor Indigo store, the Canadian flagship store, in Toronto. My literary opera was there, too, so I had twice the reason to go. Besides, I shook hands with PM Mulroney before, at the Millennium Dinner, chaired by Hon. Bill Davis. Anyway, at the book signing event the line up was so enormous, I've never seen anything like it. Heather Reisman, the CEO/owner of Indigo, introduced him. The crowd: sardines, soldiers—

have a pick.

People are attracted to power just as much as they are attracted to beauty and fame. And when we think how power and fame are being build ... Isn't that interesting? Have the right field and the right player, and history can be made. Surprisingly, not many people have the patience for the entire masquerade, otherwise we would see more power and fame on Earth."

O: "Finally, someone I can agree with. We need power and we need fame. Whatever the mask, as long as we get things done. I am a bit of an workaholic and I expect others to work hard, also. Our leaders, it's true, need more than hard working habits. They need political charms. Combination of all assets that would make a great leader are as rare as a needle in a hey stack. My eyes are wide open for a long time. Emotionally, I pray for the future of humanity."

THE FUTURE IS OURS

E: "Me, too. Some people have everything needed, yet they refuse to serve. For many intellectuals, in fact these games are not attractive—not to mention how many find the entire thing silly, even deplorable. Somehow they skip the fence of reality in their minds and let the future up for random grabs. I find that disturbing. Around the globe many countries ended up in the wrong hands because the smart capable humans refused to get involved—and even more disturbing, no one groomed the young. We need a global school designed specifically for this cause—groom smart, progressive, confident global leaders. Teach them charms also."

O: "It is happening right now from what I understand. Let me tell you, Elysse, that the political field is an aggressive psychological game. Even dangerous. No wonder many run from it."

Covered in Flowers

E: "That's why we have scientists. Find a perfect formula! Inject them with gravity."

O: "Scientists love privacy and interaction only with brilliance. Forget the ordinary."

E: "Justifiable approach, I agree—and I love them secretly for that very reason. They do not need the world. They have the universe by the tail!"

O: "Are we silly here?"

E: "Yes. Myself, I am a bit of a scientist, that's why I understand them and their needs. Writing is like science, agonizing and very detailed. Look, *The Canadian Encyclopedia,* I use, HISTORY!CA, took 20 years to assemble, the effort of some 3500 brilliant souls, and it incorporates 10 million words. Speaking of detail ..."

O: "Oh, Elysse ... You do inspire people. Now, we are on page 90, did you realize?"

THE FUTURE IS OURS

E: "I'm not suffering from fatigue yet. I could go on for a while. Let me tell you, dear Oprah, that as you intend to depart— along many other creative minds, I intend to approach the stage of performance."

O: "Is TV attracting you?"

E: "Writing attracts me. My greatest stages are and will remain, my numerous books. If that will change in the future, I could not tell, but for now I'm up to my neck in my numerous manuscripts, all to be published one after another. Sincerely, I feel love when I write. My brain hurts sometime, but I get quickly in the horizontal position to oxygenate the apparatus. Then I start all over again."

O: "Speaking of headaches, look how our generation was pushed into this unpredictable global *'spiritual exodus'* that took us for a ride for a few decades. Then filtering started. We ended up not being able to even mention God! Regardless how we put it, it was wrong, wrong, wrong. By now, at our age, we spell it out without a care."

E: "Oprah, you had a better position than most of us. The majority of baby boomers could tell you that some of our big dreams did not materialize in time. Look at me!"

O: "Better later than never!"

E: "True. Now, it is later—and it is better."

O: "You'll do fine, Elysse."

E: "What a feeling! To start so late, yet to feel like a child in paradise. I know that we, our generation, are making our splash at once, and we'll stay unified in all causes. We have grand and great-grand reasons to push for love, prosperity and global peace. It is our blood stream flowing through the billions of global children, down the galactic river. My dear Oprah. You do not have children. Kindly, I have to tell you that you do not know or feel exactly what mothers do. It takes all the pain in the world to make you a mother. Enormous pain, extended time, great sacrifice, and infinite unconditional love. My opinion is, that you made the sacrifice of not having children for the very reason that you saw the venue and the benefit of helping to inspire many of us through your permanent presence in our homes, and between so many painful lessons that we watched, here and there you injected fun in the show to make us laugh."

O: "Elysse dear, you're right. That's true. Let me tell you now that you exceeded my expectations in this imaginary interview. Our minds do blend. I thank you for the imaginary appearance on my talk show and for successfully pulverizing 25,000 words down *The Greatest Global River of Communication, AMAZON*. You have my admiration for your creativity. I also thank you for not asking what I did with the book you so beautifully packaged and sent to me from Canada on Feb. 8, 2007, as special delivery. I know it costs over a hundred dollars to do so—but, Elysse, business is risk.

From this imaginary talk show, I learned that you are a fighter! You will succeed. Much peace, love and luck in your entire future. Let me give you the most famous imaginary hug in the history of Chicago."

E: "Thank you, Oprah, for the imaginary invitation to be part of your TV talk show. Have my imaginary Canadian hug in return. We'll meet again in the future, I sense ..."

The End

Now, I feel free! Free of Oprah.

***

"Taxi! To the airport, please."

THE FUTURE IS OURS

I TURN IN BED, I CANNOT SLEEP ...
MY MIND IS TRAVELLING SO DEEP ...

I imagine the Sun as the flower of light on our
global table ...
The Moon as the candle in our global hand ...
The wind, the messenger of peace ...
The thunder, the gavel of the Creator ...
The lightning, the whip of the sky ...

It's order in the universe!

And LIFE ...

Like all humans
Who are committed to the overall greatness,
I myself find progress, very seductive.

From my corner in the field
I take the liberty to dream
The world of peace that we could build ...

It's night on Earth ...
The cloud of silence can be felt,

COVERED IN FLOWERS

I turn in bed,
I cannot sleep,
My mind is travelling so deep ...
We need the global health restored!

One dream ...
That we are being
By the Same GOD
Adored ...

Tortured by dreams of love for humanity, ELYSSE

IT'S COSMIC EVERYTHING AROUND

Before our Solar System, was a dream ...
Before LOVE, the Thrones arrived,
With magic thoughts ...

It's cosmic everything around!
From every creature, every cloud,
The sentiment of living proud
Is screaming loud.

(first part)
ELYSSE

WE MOVE THE COSMIC DUST

(last strophe)

If we dare to parachute
In fields of passion that commute,
The likelihood of growing smart
Is absolute.

My dear Global Friends, please embrace the light of the future.
Love, ELYSSE

THE HUMAN RACE DOES BLEND
MY CHARMING GLOBAL FRIEND

How wonderful it is to be human!
How divine it is to be loved ...

How intrigue plays all the reasons
Behind the dogmas and beliefs,
In the race for "Global Culture Pluralistic"
Modified in "Faith Artistic"
Who is to prevail?

Clarity is what we need!
The Creator, The Creation,

97

COVERED IN FLOWERS

Universal love for all!
A world of peace!
A home to call!
Where every human can be tall
In its nature.

All citizens of the globe! We need each other!
We need global harmony!
Agree?

Your globally relaxed poetess, ELYSSE

OUR IMPORTANCE

We are carriers of intelligence.
We see beyond this human life,
We hear the universe speak,
We listen and obey its orders.

Like dreams, like cosmic weather,
We are the ones that matter!
Designed to bring intrigue to Earth,

How clever!

ELYSSE

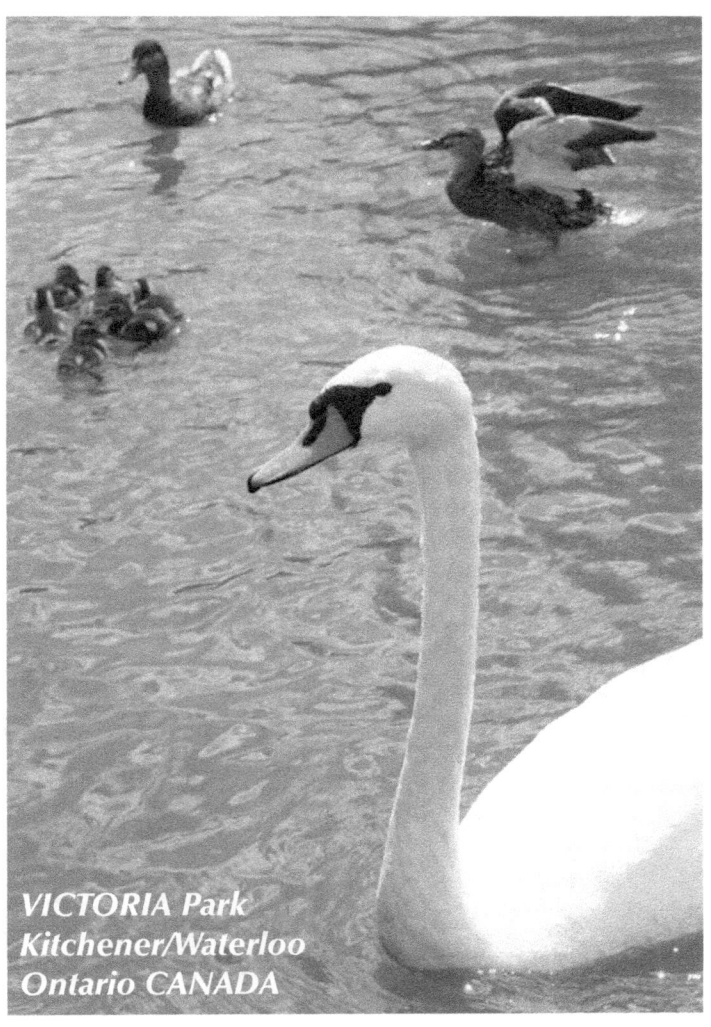

VICTORIA Park
Kitchener/Waterloo
Ontario CANADA

COVERED IN FLOWERS

On display during Elysse's book signing events in Toronto.

Chapter Two

FROM MY PERSPECTIVE,

OPRAH!

This Global Lady has talent! I say it with confidence and the feeling of security that anyone gifted with the talent to detect talent would agree. I also believe that anyone saying that the future in any way is deprived of talent could not be more wrong. Humanity has talent! ... and, *"The future is ours! Covered in flowers."* There are women and men, Oprah's age or born even earlier, who are just starting out—right across the field. How do I know? Myself, I'm one of them. I am six months older that Oprah, yet due to incredible struggles in my life, only at 47 I managed to liberate myself from the riff-raff of life's non-sense, and start on the path I deeply feel I was meant to be.

When I look around, what I see on our planet, pleasantly shocks me! Age does not mean much anymore, despite the fact that in the last decade, we, the baby boomers, were insulted and assaulted in regards to just about everything. Our age was described as a great burden on society. The economic failures was our fault. We became the scapegoats for everything that our predecessors did wrong and for the younger ones inability to grasp the idea that seriousity is needed.

Ha! Now the truth comes out about deregulation being implemented by older generations that our own. Now the truth comes out as the younger generations admitted that not only are we examples of wisdom, but we are also very funny boomers. Not only are we babes, we are boomers, also! In every sense. For example: If we did wrong, now we'll fix it. If we missed opportunities, now we'll find new ones. We raised our children, now we are free! If we missed the game of fun, now we are back in, clean and smart. ***The entire baby boomer crowd—Proud!***

Oprah is a baby boomer, just like so many of us, but unlike the majority, she was designed to enter the stage of fun and performance much younger. The ones starting now, smart people out there, are happy thinking, *'this age is a better time to start.'* Since wisdom is more present, tears will be fewer, hardship minimal, other things irrelevant, except for falling in love which can strike at any time. Easiness all the way to the finish line.

The money factor, again, is being looked at

from a totally different perspective. People focussed strictly on money are missing the point. Those who in the past hurt so many either by deceiving or insulting, calling us incompetents—look at how they are being perceived today. Mistakes were done. Many were hurt. Today, we are disarmed, but spiritually even stronger—ready to deal with the invisible future the best we can, using the instinct of trust.

Imagine existence without a shred of trust ... My advice? Always, regardless of what could be, remember the 50/50 and focus on the art of plus. Let the screen of your imagination display optimism, blessings, chance—the plus of plus, in everything.

Definitely the era of conventional broadcasting as we knew decades ago has changed and will continue to change, fast. The technological capabilities of today create competition like never before. Clearly, good communicators with balanced views will stand out. Knowledge assorted by good-will, competence, talent, sensibility and the overall wisdom to positively manipulate the global political fields, are justified demands required of anyone entering the stage of public performance. With so many billions of people on our planet and the capability to emit via satellite images and sound in every corner of the world, our ability to communicate, better be good.

We are global PR's!

'Forget the past!' I tell myself every day. *'The future is approaching fast.'* Let's not be afraid and/or fall into the trap of despair. We will succeed! I just know it. **Times come and go! We transcend them.** There will be many Oprahs in the future. Even in a world without currency, there will be famous Oprahs. She knows that. Oprah would agree with me when I'm saying that

Covered in Flowers

being famous has nothing to do with money. There are many bad, undeserving humans who have enormous amounts of money. Many criminals have more money than hard working people. Should we envy them?

No! We pity them. We wouldn't want to be them for the world. History has taught us many lessons, some very valuable.

- Mozart was and will remain famous ... yet he never was paid enough for his work.

- Rembrandt was and will remain famous ... yet he was bankrupt in his fifties.

- Nadia Comaneci was and will remain famous ... yet she was never paid properly for her talent.

These are just three examples of geniuses in their field who were not paid enough for their work—and as a consequence, suffered in every way, including insults. To this day we enjoy their music, art and images. Collectors around the world make millions and live in luxury off the very art some artists died producing. That's why '***the hungry artist***,' label is circulating freely even today, continuing to insult talents.

My husband told me a true story about a very well known German comedian who towards the end of his life was begging for food on the streets of Berlin. People, thinking that he was joking, never helped him. He died of starvation.

See how we are? Similar earthly destiny was reserved for the gentleman who built *Casa Loma* in Toronto. The same with that famous African soccer player, who we saw on BBC television recently, shot in the legs, living in a refugee camp. It breaks your heart to see him not having enough money to purchase a ticket to the *World Cup*. (Why not giving him a pension? He gave his best).

COVERED IN FLOWERS

Is this nice? Is this fair? Is this attitude something that we should preserve for the future? Oh, my friends ... We should change the future into a smarter one! A better one for all of us, all humans. As long as we permit those that do not care about anything that is decent on this planet, letting them indulge in wildly expensive lifestyles they did not work for, pain and stagnation will be the result. Work is for humans. Work is healthy. Learning is healthy. Kindness is smart.

Protection of all geniuses around the world should also be our priority. Under the umbrella of arts, they are artistic royalty.

Canada is quite advanced in the field. Numerous positive changes are taking place right now. The smart citizens blessed with financial power are stepping in. We are in the era of conscientiousness. I even read somewhere that our government intends to give serious artists, authors and musicians, a salary. That would be perfect! Imagine being able to create without worrying about your food, rent, family expenses, etc. Happy children and spouses also, even if we are up all night, creating.

These days, the baby boomers have nothing to lose, but everything to gain. They will change the world, peacefully.

Money is attractive in this life because the absence of this commodity, in general, keeps people enslaved to unnecessary silly pain and fear.

In our advanced world, around 100,000 dollars per family of four would send the stress back in its box.

Most baby boomers work part-time jobs, take part time pensions (if 60), or start new ventures attracting the young towards a new type of attitude, *'do what needs to be done.'*

COVERED IN FLOWERS

Sincerely, my heart goes to the young, who healthy as they are, have children, get stuck in hardship and society does not change as fast as it should, to alleviate the suffering of young families once and for all.

Constantly, I envision a world in which all people have plenty, without discrimination.

Would it ever be possible?
I think so. With smart, clever global leadership, anything is possible!

But no communism! Always remember how it was promoting equality for all. What a crock! That was never the case. It was worse that anyone could imagine. For many people there were no jobs. No pensions. No money. Lots of tears. Hate towards the miserable existence. Short lives. Overall, bitter memories carried generation after generation (to this day). Going back to the point, what I envision for our world is perfection! I've experienced that perfection in a few dreams that I intend to explain in a future book. In fact, my dreams along with my dramatic life provoked me to write *The Mind of a Poetess*. Every streak of rebellion and discomfort I ever felt, is in the book. Then, the global debate. I did not exclude politicians, spies or artists, courts or royales. When the book was done, even love came to me exactly as I prayed for. Oh, the finesse and sexuality I exposed in those final pages, the suspense, even paranormal.

My entire view of the world is in "The Mind of a Poetess."

Poetry is being perceived as fiction, keeping the author safe beside giving him/her the tools and the power to play with fire. And there is plenty of fire on the screen of existence that needs immediate attention. But now, I'll put it aside. Here, we continue to debate *The Oprah Phenomena*.

COVERED IN FLOWERS

Like America itself, Oprah became a symbol of a desired dream by escaping poverty.

Success! Satisfaction! She made it!

Outside my fiction, never meeting her, I could tell that she did have moments in this life when she felt alone and overwhelmed by all that came at her. Oprah has genuine spiritual sensibilities that are transcendent. I can feel her clean spirit and its restlessness.

God is her rock.

Due to the compassion she carries, often she suffers pain that others could not possibly understand or believe. If I look back I do recall how, in Chicago, from the beginning of her success Oprah many times attempted to help in so many fields where she sensed great need—and often to her surprise, the very ones in need were not responsive. We can only agree with the old saying a friend recently reminded me of:

112

THE FUTURE IS OURS

"You can lead a horse to the water—but you can not force him to drink it."

Every city has its rivers and horses. Now just imagine the variety of horses on our planet—especialy the stuborn ones who say *NO* to the fresh water of the future.

I'll live the horses in the hands of specialists at *Woodbine*, and get back to Oprah. Like all great achievers, Oprah is super-sensitive. She is spontaneous. Impulsive. These are qualities! So is her healthy ego. She needs to make decisions. Imagine not being also strong or aware of consequence. Oprah understands people. She feels their concerns and identifies with their feelings. She has a tremendous sense of self and the security in her mind's stability it's admirable. Not once did I imagine an army of people gathering information for her, compacting everything, simplifying every field, yet when it comes to the moment of entering the stage of performance, Oprah is alone. Nothing helps, nothing hurts. Like a general in the war, Oprah has to decide instantly what could save or ruin the entire show. Millions of remote controls around the world are directed at her. Click! Click!

"Now perform, my dear lady ..."

Considering the fact that she is the show, Oprah must have moments when she shakes her head in disbelieve at her own capability to manage it. Being rarity is intriguing. Being lucky feels good. Being loved cannot be described. Being watched so closely by both negative and positive armies, must be both exciting and draining, yet, Oprah displays a type of playful normality in her approach and performance. See? She was designed to be *the one*.

I know that many people watched Oprah over the years not because they liked her, but because she brought to the table subjects that no one else did—or because she asked much better questions and received broader answers. Oprah knows the viewer.

Here in Ontario, Canada, Oprah's show starts at 4:00 P.M. While I did not watch every show, I can tell you that I watched Oprah more than I go shopping or speak on the phone. There were many funny shows, smart shows, intriguing shows, dramatic shows, spiritual and inspirational shows. Not all guests invited on Oprah's show were people who inspired me (at my age), but there were plenty of them who did intrigue me with their simplicity, complexity, talent or daring attitude. Others inspired me greatly, and as a consequence, I followed them in books, on TV, in movies, at the White House, etc.

Oprah's television show was something of a "Kindle like book" that I read on a screen, in colour.

COVERED IN FLOWERS

I want you to know that I love Oprah for her talent and the effort she put to entertain me for the last two decades. I'm quite sure that many people around the world feel the same.

As a first generation emigrant, to me Oprah was like a friend with friends back home. The talk around the table. The fun. The tears. All of it!

Often, even silly things can be important to our health. Why not talk about being hurt, being sick, or abandoned? Why not debate the fact that too much external influence could be lethal, especially if it is negativity in disguise. From religions to food, from money to politics, all can influence us to a degree, push us to an extreme or another, give us a boost, or ruin us. Being child like occasionally is healthy! It's recommended. Children are flexible. Smart!

THE FUTURE IS OURS

Years ago, I went to a lung specialist because my allergies were so terrible that I ended up in the emergency room. I simply could not breathe. Anyway, above the door of that doctor's office was a huge sign printed in large bold letters, stating:

'Stress creates all allergies!'

Next, the specialist doctor scraped my arm with a multitude of allergents to see what I should avoid. Surprisingly:
- Ragweed gave me blister #1;
- Dust, blister #2;
- Detergent, #3;
- My adorable cats, tiny blister #4.

Curious, I asked the doctor about the sign above the door. Do you know what this gentleman told me? "Look, I'm 72. I am in love with my wife. I adore my cats and dogs. My garden is paradise. I could be retired, but only God knows how Ontario suffers from a shortage of lung specialists

117

Covered in Flowers

like me, that's why I decided to continue helping people like you—young and often naive in their approach to life. I love helping and positively influencing people.

Apropos, young lady, there at the reception is my natural honey, from my own bees. Take a jar. It will help you get rid of allergies resulting from pollens. Go home, love your cats, look for love or dream about it—if you are stuck in misery for now, but work towards liberating yourself from nonsense and live a life of love. Promise me?"

"Yes, Sir!"

Once out of his office, the jar of natural honey in my hand felt like a lucky charm. That man gave me a natural boost I so desperately needed. I was in my thirties then and if he was alive he would be almost 100, otherwise I would go back to show him that I followed his smart advice and I am allergy free. I breathe like a newborn baby. I am healthier than ever before and I choose to have only love in my life.

Recently, this February 2010, my male cat, LELU (a Manx) died. Oh, how I cried. From my enormous love for him and the grief of losing him, in his memory I wrote, **Forever Loved**, a bestseller on Kindle. Lelu's entire life (and his death) photographed—not to mention his special love for Mitzy, our Siamese (all in the book). Lelu and Mitzy were together since they were 4 moths old. Even now, months later, Mitzy is still grieving, calling him every day and night, "*Meow ... Meow ...*" opening every closet to see if he's hiding. It breaks my heart to see her pain.

Years ago, Lelu's veterinary doctor asked me how I came up with this name '*Lelu*.' I told him that when I was 17, back in Transylvania, I had a very young puppy (a gift). He was so adorable that I spoiled him

119

COVERED IN FLOWERS

like a baby. I named him Lelu from 'cutulelu,' meaning (in Romanian) little puppy. Wherever I went, I carried him in my arms, in my jacket or on my shoulder. When he grew a bit, he looked like the white cute puppy from the Cottonel package, with those beautiful big brown eyes.

At 19, when I moved to the city, 500 km away where I went to school, I left my two year old Lelu with my mother because it was impossible to take him with me. Not long after I left, my mother gave my Lelu away to a farmer, because she did not like very much cats and dogs. That farmer loved Lelu, but Lelu did not respond to his love. Few months later, I received a letter from my mother with the unbearable tragic news. My Lelu, displaced, without me, refused to eat. He died of a broken heart, because he loved me so ...

He refused to live without me.

THE FUTURE IS OURS

At the same time I was battling skin cancer (on my knee). A year later, a baby was killed in me. Imagine my grief! To this day, I did not completely get over the loss of my baby and my Lelu. This life is cruel!

In another book of mine called **Fertility Goddess SOVATA** I tell the story how at one point I lost five friends within two years, all young. Then, another story of how my reproductive organs stopped developing at the age of nine—and the interesting creative treatment that helped fix the nightmare, so I could get pregnant.

Regardless, I never quit school and I never gave up on hope. There is always more love, all we have to do is put the effort to accept it. I know that feeling, when the new love arrive in our home, yet we cling to the memory of the departed one. Experiencing that, I recall struggling to shake it off, to give room to the one in front of me, to let

COVERED IN FLOWERS

them feel the best of my love. It is not easy. Recovery from grief takes time.

Forever embedded in my memory is the moment I left for the city, before getting in the taxi playing with my adorable dog. Then, from the back seat waving to Lelu, who ran and ran after the taxi as he knew that I was leaving him forever. Imagine if I knew what would happen after I left. It is traumatizing to even think about it.

And now, I lost my Lelu, the cat ... only that this Lelu had a full perfect life with me in it every day of his life. This Lelu was just as happy and playful. He was also very lucky. When I adopted him from the animal shelter he was a four month old kitty, very sick, covered in dirt, rescued from a ravine. In the book I write what a beautiful life I gave him. How much I loved him. This Lelu was a gift from God after the loss of another cat, Mitzu. That's how I ended up at the shelter, looking for Mitzu, and surprisingly, come home with Lelu. It was the end of August 1997, the same time the world lost the beautiful Princess Diana. I do not know if everyone feels those energies of abdominal pain going up and down the body—assorted with excruciating turmoil that feels like a heavy stone on the chest, choking us with grief in such a horrifying way. Maybe I am super sensitive. Or maybe I am normal.

But what is normality? ***The deep desire to nurture life. That's what is normal.*** If we cannot access the button of love, we are in terrible pain. We're lost! We all have those moments. In my case, I had so much happening to me that others need to live multiple lives in order to accumulate such a mountain of extremes. Life is very interesting to watch. There is everything for everyone in it, and much more ...

Did you realize that a great number of

people with wealth, for example, have never experienced true love. They go public and tell it. Many people actually have no clue how true love feels. They can imagine in a variety of ways, but it is never like the reality of feeling true love for someone— and being truly loved. Even I didn't know what it was like until 2004, at age 49.

That fairy tale concept of ultimate spiritual excitement is almost everyone's ultimate dream—and that cannot be bought.

To be forced to choose between love and money, we have plenty of examples of what people end up choosing ...

Love! Of course!

What I believe, is the fact that if you have love, money can be made without too much frustration. People in love agree almost completely on everything. They work well together and they prefer to be together, always. They hold hands even in their sleep. Sometimes they have to part because the pain of love is unbearable. When they touch—it hurts with love!

Just a few years ago I would have been amused at such proposals. Now I regret to know that humanity overall does not have the privilege. In 2001 my muses of inspiration told me that *it will happen*, soon. I cannot wait to see humanity suffering from the pain of love—the greatest gift of all.

Through history, not once did royalty give up the throne for love, never regretting it.

Here, skeptics can debate forever! But, what do they know? Being struck by love is just as rare as being struck by luck or lightning. It is very, very rare. That's why many will never understand, unless they get it.

The army in love—agree with me.

COVERED IN FLOWERS

Sincerely, I wish I had super powers. It hurts me not to be able to strike at once the entire planet with these out of this world divine energies, so full of finesse ... yet a type of *'love pain'* that makes you cry ... From my infinite desire to help humanity, I burst with creativity in *The Mind of a Poetess*, when I call these energies the *Refined Fire*. In the book, I managed to empower the entire human race. Like Oprah, my duty on Earth is to empower people through my writings and through art in general.

My clean mind and dreams of progress are my greatest gifts to humanity.

I believe that Oprah had an extraordinary influence on the global society. She broke barriers that even her male predecessors could not. She worked mentally, which is much harder than physical work. Absorbing stress the way she did and not falling apart, denotes great mental strength. No one could train or prepare someone for this role or that role. It is either there—or it is not! Practice in any domain can only do one thing—It makes it better.

Oprah has a unique gift from God. She also has 'the awareness' and the ambition to use it to its fullest capacity. From my humbled perspective, she has surpassed all expectations. Oprah goes down in my history as 'My 4:00 pm Entertainment Tablet.'

The End

COVERED IN FLOWERS

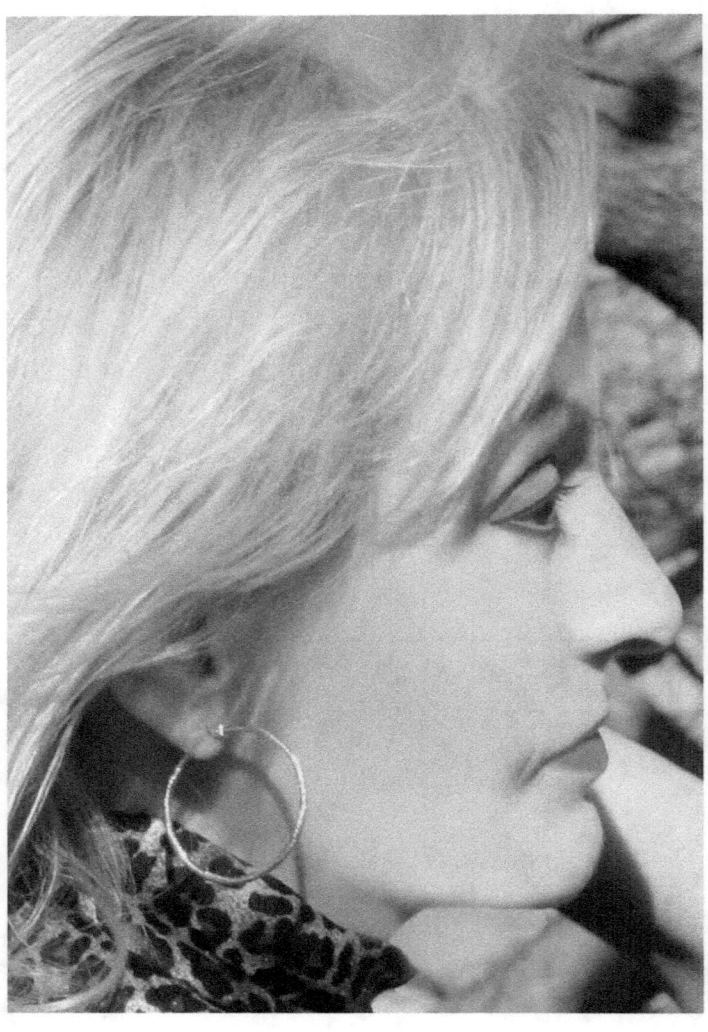

Chapter Three

REALITY VS THEATRICS
BABY BOOMERS' DIFFERENCES
ELYSSE
VS
OPRAH

My dear friends, Oprah successfully entertained me for many years and I sincerely regret to see her depart. Because of her talent to promote openess and because of her show guests, the so

129

many humans who confessed their lives, even I managed to relax a bit, thinking, *"We are all troubled humans, occasionally."* The multitude of guests deserve lots of applause, as there would have never been an Oprah show without the guests' brilliant participation.

Actors are actors, we see them everywhere from every corner, sometimes too much, but here I'm talking about the ordinary people who gave Hollywood great competition with their natural talent to entertain—and made Oprah more money than most famous actors did for Hollywood's entertainment business.

Like I said, being born six months earlier than Oprah, over the years I often fantasized of being on her show, to be able to compare notes. Like Oprah, I'm gifted with incredible memory, curiosity, and the talent to describe events, tell stories, write incred-

The Future is Ours

ible poetry, photograph beauty beyond imagination—and I believe that an opportunity to have a dialog with her would have been a very entertaining, tender feminine baby-boomer moment. It would have been *comedy a la carté.*

Example: Recall when Oprah explained to all of us how as children they were instructed to get under the desks in case of a nuclear war? Atomic bomb falling on USA?

Oh, my ... I don't know about you, in your countries, but behind the so-called '*iron curtain,*' no such preparations took place. As children, we were very concerned. We could see the adults listen secretly to the **BBC Radio program** called **Free Europe**, which was illegal in Romania, and we were afraid! My mother would lock the doors and whisper, "*Shush! Listen ... Jesus is coming! Apocalypse is here. The end is here.*"

COVERED IN FLOWERS

Some cruel adults would say to us:
"Get over it! We are forever squashed
between Ivan and The West,
like a helpless puppy.

If a bomb comes, we are all toast!
It would be very fast and easy—like a
quick needle in the tooshy. Now go and
have an apple! ... and stop wondering."

Others would fantasize what would happen if the Chinese would just walk over Europe. Of course, because of their incredible large numbers, people laughed! ... and said:

"If these locusts only pass over our tiny
country, who needs a bomb? All they have
to do is, just eat all our food supplies and
we would die of starvation! A very slow,
painful death. The entire Europe would
also be forever deprived of cats and dogs."

As a child I felled like digging a secret

hole in the ground and hide some of my hazelnuts, candy—and my cat and dog.

All these stories that I carry in my super-clean memory, I'll dispense of them as I go, one at a time, in future writings that I'm in the process of publishing. Horrible events, scary moments, comic descriptions, I carry them all. Comedy is the butter of history.

Teenage German boys slaughtered and their corpses scattered all over the place. Their white shirts hanging from the forest trees. Smaller children, my mother includ-ed would walk between corpses saying: *"This is Fritz—This is Hantz. This is Thomas—This is Martin."* Some uncles who died young of war injuries told other tragic stories. One of them was about Jewish vir-gin girls aligned on the banks of the Black Sea and shot dead to fall of the cliffs, washed by the water influx ... Most women during the war were so scared that they painted their faces with chalk, as so many Russian soldiers were raping like in the movie *Rambo*. Raped, abused, only skin and bone, many women, traumatized, continued living—but strictly for the children, like robots. Suicide would have been very easy, but it was evil to abandon the children again and again. Infinite cases all over. Adults of all nationalities: Romanian, German, Hungarian, Jewish, Slavic, Greeks, Gypsies, etc., all crying on each other's shoulder. All survived the same dark inexplicable evil. No one was spared! When evil took over Romania in the end, it stayed there camouflaged and active. It took half a century to clear the waters of darkness.

In my family I had all nationalities. My family members did marry Germans and Hungarian, and my grandfather from my mom's side married a Hungarian lady, the widow of a Jewish man. Her five children left for Israel, but she refused to go. She was deeply in love with my grandfather and both lived well into their nineties. From them alone I learned a great deal about sincere love, strength, calm, smart work and a peaceful clean life. They were moderate Christians, not fanatics—and they made love physically until the last moment of life. My step-grandma, Aniko, died at 94 of pneumonia. After she died my grandfather was waking up at night and searching for her. He died three months later, at 96, of broken heart and grief. (My real grandmother, my mom's mother (mother of 10), died in her fifties, in a traffic accident).

See? Dear ladies and gentleman, the global stories in a few phrases, not even developed and are still good. Now imagine me telling detailed stories. Most people do not have the appetite to sit down and do it. They get very frustrated. When you start a book, after a while for many it becomes very hard to continue. The amount of detail needed to develop a good story kills the appetite of those who dream of writing. You can hear people saying, "I have it all sorted out in my head—I just need someone to put it together for me."

Oh, oh ... Do these people realize that good writers are slaves to the ART?

Myself, I wouldn't do it for others, probably, even if paid big money. The pressure on my brain is not visible, yet after I'm out of the trance of writing I often feel pain. Carrying such vocabulary at my fingertips and being able to structure properly everything, is quite phenomenal. Really! I love it, and I feel enormously blessed to be able to handle modern English and the closest descendant to Latin in this fashion. For the future, I can confidently suggest:

Get the best out of me!

THE FUTURE IS OURS

Indulge in the European and Canadian literary cuisine. You'll be satisfied, I guarantee. I'll ad all the gravy needed to please my readers. I love pleasing. It pleases me.

Under the umbrella of this great spirit, called Elysse Poetis, I promise to entertain humanity for as long as I live. All my life I promised God in my prayers that I would do just that if he would be so kind and give me the gift of writing. Mainly, I prayed for talent and love. These days I pray for everything and everyone.

By now, it is clear to me that some people are designed to talk, others to write, others to have lots of children, some to be leaders or any other profession in existence. Regardless, we all need love. We all love to cook and eat elegant food. Some of us love reading everything. So, when I imagine two women of the same age, Oprah and Elysse, from two different continents, yet neighbours for the last 28 years, in my mind this is pure theatre. Just imagine!

Canada vs US
2 Baby Boomers—Theatrical Debate

Engaged in a balanced debate over the last five decades of memories would have delivered some justice to the hundreds of millions of Europeans who are still carrying the trauma of the two greatest wars in the history of humanity. Many of them citizens of Canada and US, for decades. There are plenty who never stoped grieving.

Only now, as usual after more than sixty-five years from the events, we see here in Canada in special TV documentaries the tens of millions killed in Europe.

Small adorable children dressed up for kindergarten, laying in the streets of Frankfurt, killed by bombs. The children of England and Ireland taken away ...

138

THE FUTURE IS OURS

At least in Western Europe the events are on tape. In Eastern Europe, maybe, no such documentaries exist. The whisper always remained the same in regards to the enormous loss of life during and immediately after the greatest two world wars—approximately 51,000,000 deaths. Besides, let's never forget that we arrived at this point in history on the shoulders of even more millions who throughout history died for our freedom, success, development and peace.

Pillow talk for those our age is therapeutic. My husband and I compare notes all the time. We were both born after the war, he in Germany, Frankfurt—me in Romania, Sibiu. Right there we have perfect examples of *Democracy vs Communism*. Along the debates we have a lot of fun, too. We even laugh at the shortage of food (for a while) in our years of development. *"We could have been taller,"* we argue.

Covered in Flowers

We also subscribed to German TV to see what is going on in Europe these days, socially, economically, intellectually, culturally and mainly technologically.

Wow! Sincerely, we are impressed. Those people are so powerfully creative and clean that it is shocking! In 1980, I lived in Germany, near Stuttgart, for about three months, then I lived in Austria for seven months. In fact as a child I even attended German music classes. All my neighbours were German. In my experience Germans are very kind people. No wonder so many famous stars marry them and went to live there. When I married my German husband, after a while I started crying at the realization of my enormous luck. How can he be so kind and gentle? ... so clean, so loving and, of course, such an extraordinary cook.

Germans are second in the world when it

comes to cooking, right after French. They have people from all over the world training there. The monks and nuns are in charge with the beer and schnaps. It is so much fun watching the German cooking shows—and 'Clever,' of course, (a scientific show). Speaking of science, are these people ever advanced in technologies and kind enough to share their knowledge with the world. They do have cosmic friends, we're being constantly informed. Muses ...

My husband and I, learned a lot from each other. Our life is that of a fairy tale— something I could only imagine in my dreams. Yeah, here I am lucky in both, the love sector and the creative sector. This is superior! I am very, very happy. I feel very blessed. It is the very extreme I could only dream of. And now, these days, here I am, living it.

Ladies and Gentlemen, Go find love ...

141

Covered in Flowers

Read my entire struggle in my search for love and even my arguments with God. You can call this force anything you want, but trust me that it is there for all of us, available through faith. This force gives us the free will and the drive to engage in action.

Faith is in fact trust.

Deep trust in possibility.

That's what I believe.

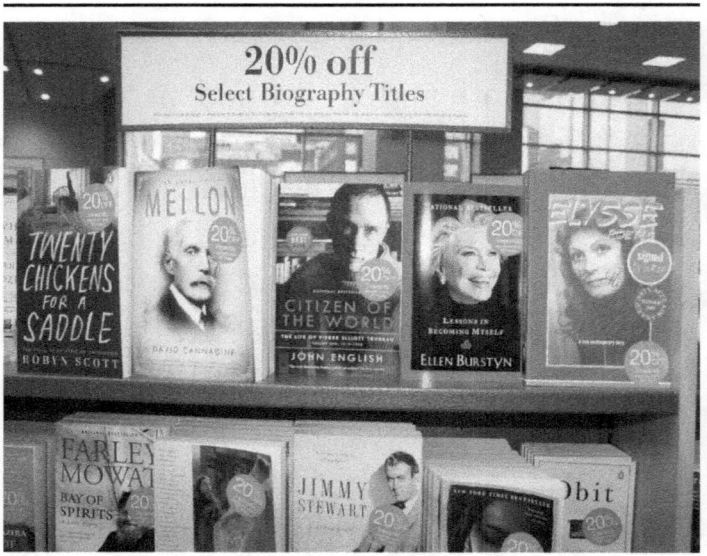

COLLISION OF IDEAS

In the world of creation ideas colide!
And there isn't a question crossing my mind
About the truth overlapping,
The reason of trapping,
Prolonging debates, provoking discord ...

Oh, my dear globals,
We no longer afford to prolong stagnation!
Today "The Global Nation"
Needs just two things my friends!
CLARITY & CAUSE

***

Psst! can you hear that?
Let's listen with patience
To the divine applause
Comming towards Earth
From other cosmic nations ...

My friends, prepare to stay engaged in this cosmic ride.

ELYSSE

COVERED IN FLOWERS

In my first book I stated: "*I do believe that I do hold, the pen of gold.*" With this pen of gold, I wrote so much that I could not stop. My editorial team cut in half the original scripts, and even so *The Mind of a Poetess* remained quite big at 432 pages. In the revised version I promise not to go after the editor and change certain things. All silly errors are my fault. But the content of the book is out of this world.

During my book tour I was competing for attention with *Harry Potter* and *The Secret*. Even so I had success. Actually many readers told me that *The Mind of a Poetess* is it. More clear, detailed and empowering.

Great writers are very special creatures—sensitive and complex. Not everyone understands them. Like scientists, writers are in their own world. Poets, oh poets ... They are super-sensitive and at times child-like, fragile spirits—loving spirits.

The Future is Ours

Some of us love reading. We read a lot and very fast. We read everything and everyone. We are very curious about everyone's experience and opinion. We do not change our opinion in order to compliment anyone else's, but we believe that it is good to know how people think. It intrigues us!

When I'll go to God, I'll tell Him how all the *O Magazines* I read if put together would be bigger than *The Mind of a Poetess,* which my imaginary friend, Oprah, did not read yet. Or maybe I'm wrong! Maybe she did! In February 2007. Winters are for reading! But, she lives in California.

Anyway, Oprah is promoted in my books and so are many other famous names, people I love watching, following in arts, politics, etc. Without modesty, convinced I am of one thing—that it will come a day when everyone in the world will love to read Elysse. I know it. I feel it. I dreamed it.

IN LOVE WITH THE POLITICIAN

(continued from ...)

The price is immense
The ardour intense
The atmosphere tense;

No love for us ever ...
No chance!

That's it! It is clear!
No reason to cry in past tense.
But let's just imagine no prohibition,
Nor the sharks of opposition
With the ever dark ambition
To ruin ...

Regardless,
I'll hold that feeling, so supreme ...
Your eyes filled with fire
Of love and desire
Forever will spark in my dream.

I'll burn flames with fire!
Chain love, with its wire!

THE FUTURE IS OURS

Stop the dream with your fame,
In the name of the game.

To all politicians in the world:
Smell the flowers of your powers
In the garden of your fame.
Stay safely loved.

Sir ... Madam ... Smart Global Leaders ...
I bow to you ...
... as I EXIT your secret pain of restrictions ...

Your politically correct poetess, illusive, ELYSSE

See what I mean? How I turn everything into art. Decent, fun art. People pay big bucks for sport events, yet many find books expensive. Many authors suffer losses and stagnation, discouragement and insult, instead of compensation for their efforts. Look how some of the greatest of our times in fiction were refused and ignored—yet, years later when the public discovered them, magic happened! Authors Stephen King and J. K. Rowling are best examples. These two very competent authors were ignored and refused by some of the best in the field of publishing. *"No! No! No!"* is what they heard over and over again, until the day when 'that special moment' arrived, and all green lights turned on for them, at once.

Judge Judy said it right on Larry King not long ago when the media went bananas over Anna Nicole Smith. Judge Judy asked Larry: "What did she do? Why all this attention? Did she write a book? Did she discover something?"

"Bravo, Judge Judy. I like it!" We can only agree with Judge Judy and with David Foster. Many do not deserve to be so powerfully promoted on TV, especially if they did not produce anything smart, or they produce bad meaningless and negative provocative art/lyrics, and behave badly on top of everything—then go on the air to reason their wrong doing. There are some true deceivers out there. No one escaped them in this life—not even smart talk shows.

Let me return to Anna Nicole. In my opinion she was a loving mother, a struggling soul in need of security and love which she never had the privilege to find, except in her children and Howard Sr., whom she loved strictly for loving and protecting her and her young boy. Sadly, nothing helped, and she died of grief when her boy died.

Books ... Books. In 2001, when I filed for divorce, I did not go on medication or purchase alcohol to numb myself. I do not consume any toxins nor do I like bars, discos, religious extremism, promiscuity, bad language or malicious gossip. What did I do?
I purchased books worth
$10,000

Covered in Flowers

Many of these books were on sale, except for a few encyclopedias/dictionaries that are indispensable in my creative environment. I also went to garage sales and found good old books I so much love, mainly because they were published long ago, reflecting those times. These days all valuable books are on Amazon.

For the first few months I just read day and night, often crying. One day, out of the blue, muses of inspiration took over my mind. Creativity overwhelmed me. The rest is history. I never stopped writing since. I'm privileged! Look, I can write!

Muses of inspiration do exist!
Voices and energies are those muses.
Mediums, if you wish—like in science.
You feel it. They touch and console you.

Who never had the experience cannot possibly imagine. It is so beautiful, intriguing—in the beginning shocking and scarry.

THE FUTURE IS OURS

COVERED IN FLOWERS

Most creative minds on Earth mention dreams, voices or other forms of experiences present prior to their best moments of creativity. Musicians are just as intrigued. People like me, who do not use anything but mainly healthy food and water, have a very clear understanding that something beyond human comprehension is at work. And it is a miracle! I see it that way.

Have you heard of so many humans all over the world trying anything in order to find their chi, meaning these special energies? (the abdominal pain of excitement).

Here, in North America, people call it *fire in the belly.* Remember Mary Lou Retton in the *1984 LA Olympics*? She gave everyone fire in the belly with her charming smile alone. Julia Roberts in *Pretty Woman*? She stirred the fire in the belly around the world. Michael Jackson, similar story. Miss Monroe with her beauty, the same. Then the

THE FUTURE IS OURS

Kennedy brothers with their magnetism. President Clinton with his charm. Princess Diana with her royal beauty and elegance. More recently, President Obama who shares similarities with Tom Cruise when he smiles ... and destiny *'Trust'* shared with Princess Diana, Marlon Brando, Sidney Poitier, Michael J. Fox, Calvin Klein, George Clooney, and others.

Oprah's destiny is *'Mastery'*—same as John Travolta's. That's why they get along.

Me? My karmic path is *'Electricity*!' I share my path with Einstein, Elvis Presley, William Faulkner, writer, winner of Nobel Price for literature, etc. I love my karma! I am a Leo II, blessed with considerable strength, balance and vision to instigate needed changes. I'll leave a legacy that will last for generations, I'm being told. And there are many more good things about me. All I have to do is shake the world, as

COVERED IN FLOWERS

Einstein and Elvis did. Do not expect me to spike my hair or shake my booty. That's not going to happen. I am quite conservative in nature.

Seriously, how did I discovered this extraordinary information? When I purchased books worth $10,000, my daughter also gave me a $250 gift certificate. So, she suggested that I purchase *The Secret Language of Destiny*, to learn a bit about my place in this life, my purpose. Authors, Gary Goldschneider and Joost Elffers. Nine years ago I paid for their book $45, and I never regret it. I love this book! In fact I'm so in love with books that I fantasize about the most elegant library on Earth, all mine. I can only imagine *The Royal Library*.

Look! The book is on *www.amazon.com* for convenient prices. Trust me, this is a very good book to have in the house, along with my books, of course. I recommend

THE FUTURE IS OURS

The Secret Language of Destiny because it is fun, smart, scientific. It stimulates the mind and provokes you. Helps.

Speaking of destiny, do you know that in communism astrology was prohibited? I've never seen a horoscope there and I didn't even know that I was a lioness until I came to Canada. Two things I learned from a lady who was, I suppose, a secret astrologer to the secret service: reading in black coffee and reading in cards. With my good memory I picked up the craft instantly, but I never practiced it. Nor I ever again consumed Turkish Coffee and I do not keep any playing carts in my environment. For some reason anything of that sort gives me the shivers—I do not like it.

Back to the young lady, in fact, this beauty had four children from four different secret service officers. She was protected and loved by all four, who on the other hand were happily married men. It was shocking to me. For sure she was sent in my environment to spy on me before I left Romania, but she became attached to me, having fun and friendly normal conversations. She never did any damage to me, but again, I was clever enough not to mention to her anything about my secret plan, my life, my intentions. I just played silly, like a normal girl would.

Oh, how happy I am to be here!

Right at the beginning, after being in Canada for just a few months, across from my apartment door was living a young couple with a baby. The young mother was baby sitting for a friend, just as I was doing. My child was only a few months old and so was the baby I was looking after. Every day, when the friend would arrive to pick up her baby from my neighbour, these two young women would hold long and loud conversations, disturbing my babies which some-times were asleep.

You know how it is when you've had enough. Courageous, I opened my door and asked them to go inside the apartment and talk, not in front of my door.

Wow! What a mistake.

Being new immigrants themselves, from Portugal, these young ladies did not detect my accent, so they called me, '*Stupid Canadian*.' At the time I was not a Canadian citizen yet, but this was a promising begin-ning. "One day I'll be legitimate," I thought. That was a sweet/bitter moment.

Look how here, in North America, we arrived from all over the world. We share the space and its resources—not only the natural, but also the spiritual.

We share recipes ... We fall in love ...
We marry each other ...

I LOVE OUR NOBLE QUEEN

We become global!

We are the most mixed continent on the planet. My own North American family has it all—including 'The Mongolian Spot.' That's why I believe that we, humanity, can have a wonderful future if we accept once and for all that we are family, all of us, together. Let's stop pushing silly buttons!

Global commerce is extremely important to progress. So are languages. We all share the English language along with hundreds of other secondary languages. We are a force that cannot be compared with any other forces in the history of humanity.

America has never suffered a shortage of admirers. It never will.

Re-inventing fashionable arts that could keep humanity engaged with curiosity, and globally safe, is crucial! The up-coming history can be easily manipulated in favour of global peace through the innocent 'art channels.'

Culture is art. Art creates change.
In a culture improved—Art is the heart.
Science rules overall—universally!

Oprah will forever be preserved in my mind as a talented artist, a narrator of global events (fun events, or drama), the voice of unity. All these years, she just knew how to connect and by putting herself in everyone's shoes she gained the trust of people. Many gladly confessed their happiness or devastation to her. Oprah did excellent in the majority of circumstances.

Life goes on ... Many are interested and strong enough to enter the game of leadership and communication, and preserve the flow of intelligence needed to feed society. I am convinced that we will do not only good, but very good in the next few years. We need to change the world—and fast.

COVERED IN FLOWERS

CNN's "Keeping Them Honest," with Anderson Cooper is a best example. Plus many others. I like what I see.

How many times did we asked ourselves: Where in the universe can decent humans find fairness and respect—when lust, theft, financial crime, illegal pyramids made legal, and corruption, continue to plague humanity—and criminals commit all sorts of evil against the innocent, right across the globe.

How many people do we think see it this way? How many are simply revolted at the so called 'smart advisors,' who called everyone stupid from their high thrones of deceit. Like the religious extremists, so were the monetary extremists—luring people to invest, then pushing them out of their homes all over the world, insulting the seniors, provoking many formerly accomplished middle class professionals to commit suicide, no different than those desperate farmers in India or the assembly workers in China. Did you see that on TV?

We have to be smart and careful. Let's pray that a credit crunch will never hit these two gigantic nations. (The damage could be greater than that of an atomic strike). Let's not forget, when you force the chick out of the egg prematurely, the chick does not survive. I've seen it as a child. Last year India had over 60,000,000 millionaires. (If Canada would have that, every child, senior, teenager and adult would be millionaires). That's a lot. China, who knows?

Pure democracy evolving in these countries of billions, in the beginning could be excitement. Credit applications flying all over, no different than those silver ribbons thrown out of the airplanes in Eastern Europe during the communist propaganda. As a child, too young to understand, I used to run and pick them up from all over the fields, and played with them. In recent years, as an adult, the credit offers reminded me of those ribbons.

At the global level, there is no difference between the human feeling. Humanity needs relaxation, respect, trust and love. Security in a tomorrow, appreciation, a good future for all, including animals and nature. Tribal societies need political and social upgrading to the level of democratic societies, for the good of it all. From what I see, the process of upgrading has began.

Revolt is not on my mind,
but what I do promote is,
ORDER for the 21st Century.

A common, inclusive type of global order that makes sense and eradicates illiteracy, criminality, sickness, hunger and suffering. A type of order that empowers all good

162

global citizens and gives them easy access to resources, to good commerce.

Out with the devil!

The future should be clean.

Like Mozart, a husband and a father of three children who suffered financially, or Rembrandt who was bankrupt in his 50's—the global charmer President Clinton and his beautiful and intelligent lady, US Secretary of State Hilary, also suffered financial crises before becoming super-wealthy. Today, look how much 'the receptive ones' around the globe would pay Mr. Clinton or Mr. Blair for their speeches.

See? Communications and smarts mixed with compassion and understanding. I love it! I love it! We are progressing nicely.

About finances?

This phenomena, 'financial anemia,' is

plaguing over 90 percent of humanity at any given time. So, why condemn? We have to be careful what we say. Push respect up front! Make the people feel appreciated. They are the bees bringing home the pollen to make this life sweet. Give them clean fields, beauty, clean air, safe environments from where they can produce—where they can enjoy freedom and have fun multiplying. Be regal!

Now I feel like I'm talking to the aliens, who would have all these powers. If they do, let's hope they listen and help.

However, I'll continue. Improvement is a infinite duty. How do we know that our planet is not a primitive one out there in the galaxy? Which would automatically make us all small entities in the face of other cosmic nations. Could it be that we are unable to even comprehend the meaning of rich or poor in the universe? What is it?

THE FUTURE IS OURS

We all shall remember that in the near future the currency of today will not exist—or—we could be the first planet in the galaxy made of 100% millionaires.

See? Now we have it! That's what is going to happen! Planet Earth will be the millionaires planet. It is possible! Just think about it! If a family of five from Niagara decide to fly into space, at $200,000 a ticket, they need to be millionaires. Now we know! Our leaders kept secret from us the yummy news. Regardless, let's stay happy.

Now, we are talking about the devil who is insulting humanity, race by race, for far too long. Humans from all nations were sold for money in the past, and to this day human trafficking continues for prostitution, body parts, slavery or trophies. Children and poor families from around the world are the most vulnerable targets and not much is being done to save them.

COVERED IN FLOWERS

Motive? The devil is too big. Who cares! It's not our business. Dangerous field. I'm not getting involved. Danger!

Shame! Isn't it? This aspect of our human race reflects on our inability to create order, implement respect, protect the vulnerable, take care of our youth and our global children. In our world we eat plates of food so big—they would feed an entire family for a week in another country. Some of us feel guilt and shame. How many times do we cry seeing the images of devastation—children and animals only skin and bone, abandoned, crying, hungry or tortured? How often did we hear from 'some' around us:

"Do not look—Do not cry.

Do not watch—Do not pay attention.

Do not listen—There is nothing we can do."

Really? As I advance in age, I realize that I have pain in my being by just observing the field of life. This pain does not go away. Here I'm spelling it out for the world to hear. It makes me question our integrity as healthy advanced humans.

Where is the God in us? The powerful force that we inherited as a gift, for free. Shouldn't we put that force to work and save our future from devastation? Are we just spectators, like primitives, putting the roosters and the dogs kill each other, so we can have fun? Are we returning to Roman times, pushing gladiators into the rings with lions? I hope not!

We watch earth quake victims being re-victimized by the false promises of hope. Money donated disappearing without trace. Thieves getting rich off the backs of victims. Governments so young in the concept of governing that it takes them forever to accomplish progress. Poor countries killing with drugs the young of wealthy countries.

COVERED IN FLOWERS

Where is Rambo?

We really need to clean the planet ASAP. Can we do it? Should it be done?

What else is there that we could do?

Millions of things can actually be done in a very elegant, pleasant way, without the human Rambo. Let him get married, have children and live a happy life. Remember, right now our young men and women are our Rambos. That will change in the very near future. Pain and suffering will be eradicated. Prosperity and peace will prevail—I trust. *"It will be wedding in the universe ... tomorrow night ..."* I wrote and I dream ...

Sincerely, lets look at ourselves, our spiritual resources and our greatest God given gifts *'love and the free will'*—and use them right. Yes, we can change the world in a smarter one. We need to be presentable and prepared with a smart and elegant

THE FUTURE IS OURS

human portfolio when we will be invited along other cosmic nations to make our presentation *"At The Galactic Table,"* (poem). We have to improve our chances of progress in the galaxy. We need friends all over the universe. We need to not only survive, but to progress and enjoy our existence among other cosmic nations.

Can we do it? Do we have the intelligence available, needed to succeed?

Yes! We can—if we accept complexity.

Most recently, everywhere and on Oprah, the shows about Sarah *The Duchess of York* also made me think deeply.

Isn't there anyone to give her a shoulder? I'm positive that millions of smart humans who were watching TV channel after TV channel reporting the incident, did not think much about it, until it escalated to the last straw. That's when from around the world people responded, defending Sarah.

Most did find terrible cruelty in the entire thing. First, a deceiver luring The Duchess. Then the tape which was obtained with evil intent being played over and over again, traumatizing her. Vulnerable beyond normality, not aware that once again she was in the wrong place at the wrong time, as she was crying the tears she never had time to cry in earlier years, for losing her parents, then the rest of her stability, why not suggest to her, like criminal lawyers would, and push her into admittance that she is the ultimate failure, morally and spiritually bankrupt. Take in consideration that parallel *The Duchess* was honoured for her volunteer work (Children in Crisis charity).

My questions are: As a world, are we enjoying abusing the ones around us? Why are there so many who have no problem throwing stones at Sarah or others?

THE FUTURE IS OURS

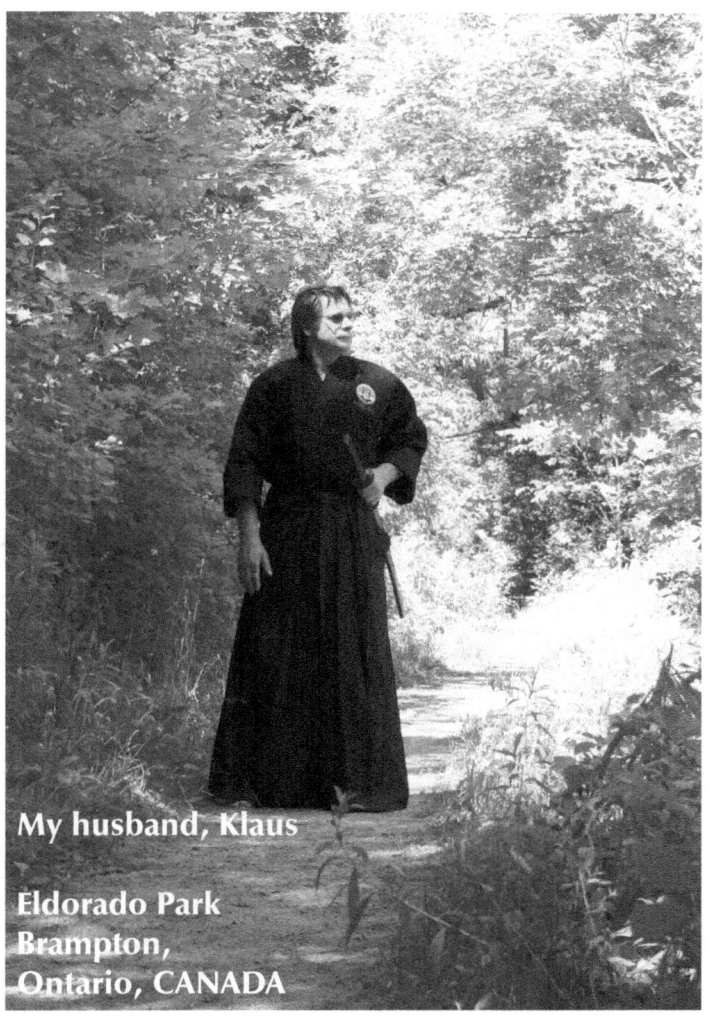

My husband, Klaus

Eldorado Park
Brampton,
Ontario, CANADA

COVERED IN FLOWERS

Comparing to many public figures out there, Sarah is angelic—a high spirited young lady who never harmed anyone, who many would feel more that happy to have her in their company. Considering her childhood, Sarah did wonderful! She loves art. She writes books. She is a superb communicator. She is kind. She is a wonderful loving mother. By now a elegant, fashionable lady I enjoy watching.

Sarah, The Duchess, has her gifts from above: God made her royal. Her daughters are princesses. Unlike many, she has her place in history, in the *Royal Library* along her books, forever.

With all my love, admiration and respect for Oprah, here I have to admit my discomfort. When Sarah cried—I cried. Why? Let's see! Right now around the world even billionaires are depressed for losing enormous amounts of money. Remember the German billionaire who last year committed suicide? We all watched Michael Jackson's brother saying on CNN that he believes Michael was killed. Why didn't Michael have enough to pay his debts? Money, money, money—again and again. Those who invested in Dubai lost billions—yet life goes on. People start over. Isn't that normal?

Soon we'll have more billionaires on Earth than ever! We'll go shopping around the world in minutes. *Technologies are so advanced that space and time travelling are here, now.* Other planets are already waiting for our arrival. Real estate all over the galaxy is up for grabs. Asteroids are giving us more minerals, gold and diamonds than we could possibly handle. We have technologies beyond the simple mind's comprehension.

Humans are the solid gold! Humans are the fortunes in the universe, not money.

173

COVERED IN FLOWERS

While watching in disbelieve, I was thinking, "This cannot be real. Why would the human race be so cruel? Even Oprah, she never did this before!" To see Sarah cry ... fragile ... yet, preserving her elegance ...

This was the last blow to her and I did not like it. Money, money, money. I could not help but think how Her Majesty, *The Queen*, absorbed the pain of her granddaughters. Those two young princesses dearly love their mother, Sarah. We parents know that. By now, I am convinced that only those of us who have children correctly understand that pain. The deeper the love, the deeper the pain. When we give life to our children, we give birth to perfect love and pain.

Can we imagine how many humans alive right now will leave everything behind and start over? How many will die instantly, and leave their huge amounts of money to God knows who? How many would pay anything to save themselves from incurable diseases? How many of us arrived here empty handed, without a home or family, food to eat, or a language to speak?

Myself, I learned that overall in existence beyond this life, money means nothing—zero! In my numerous near death experiences, out of this body I did not have money, yet I was so fine ... so happy ... totally free, and me.

I'm one of those humans who started from zero a few times, regardless of my smart discipline. My destiny took the control out of my hand. I recall my last night in (then) the notorious refugee camp Traiskirchen, near Vienna (in 1981)—I slept beside a pool of human blood. We were hundreds, like sardines, all sleeping in the same room, fully dressed. Beside my two level bed, someone was killed right there and no one

Covered in Flowers

washed the floor beside my bed. Security kept the lights on all night because theft, killings and assassinations were common. Being five and a half months pregnant, hungry, emotional, I stared all night into the DNA of that blood and prayed for the victim. It smelled alive.

In the morning, as we were prepared to fly all over the world in our adoptive countries, I embarked on the Austrian Airline along with approximately 300 Polish refugees who were running from the Martial Law in Poland, and we all left Europe forever. As we were flying over the Atlantic I could not but be amazed at the sight of so many babies hanging in the little swings above the seats in a smoke that could have been cut with a knife, and none of them were crying.

Interesting times. Forever good reminders. To this day, I believe that Traiskirchen has needy refugees who face deadly moments, come face to face with assassins, receive death threats—like me! And we cry over a commodity that cannot buy happiness, health, tranquility, freedom, love or peace.

It's true that money can help us build faster the future, but what use can money be if we are at each other's throats? ... and mentaly enslaved to materialism?

The rich die just as scared and unaccomplished as the poor ones. I could also argue that many so called rich ones, in reality are the poorest souls out there! The lights are on, but nobody's home—zero intellect. A smart poor person comes out on top any minute. In fact, many intelligent people are totally disgusted with the showing off incompetents who, some of them, made their fortunes through corruption, or just happened to be at the right place at the right time, lucky, or inherited fortunes they

177

did not sweat for. (Luck does exist, I learned).

After the collapse of communism, in 1989, I recall a Oprah show about the devastated orphans in Romania. She even asked, "What can I do to help?" Like anywhere else, example Haiti, often interference is invasive. Even I could not do much, except for the financial help. My sister had 4 children and before the revolution her husband was forced to build the marble steps in the government palace for free. With great humour I recall a time when I sent a package full of condoms to my sister, and the secret service confiscated the goods. I can only imagine the fun they had.

While shopping in 2001, on the front cover of a magazine I spotted something about a Romanian lady and Oprah. I purchased the magazine without reading carefully, only to arrive at the ranch and realize that was some controversy going on in regards to Oprah's name being used for a web site.org. In those days I was dreaming of writing to Oprah about my good spirit, my fashionable global mind.

"Nah!" I said to myself. *"I'll have to become a Scarlet. Dig for my own carrots of success in the ground of possibility— and swear to God! To never go hungry again!"*

But let me tell you that even I've found some inappropriate attachments to my name since I entered the writer's world. I always remind myself, *"It is not the nationality—It is the individual, the spirit in that person."* I've meet people from every corner of this world, good, elegant in manners, healthy in their vision, angelic overall. Then we have within our own families one or two who want us dead. Let it be clear that good people are mixed very well with the negative ones, all over the planet. Speaking

179

of order, it is not easy to police everyone.

Wouldn't it be much easier and fun if education would be available for free, main stream globally? And the ones who refuse theoretic education to be given other alternatives, via skills—shown on a sky-belt screen rotating around the globe?

Scientists, take NOTE: Images in the sky could speed up the progress.

And so, the Sarah story made me sad. When someone is on their knees, waving the white flag, we just do not shoot them. We help!

Billy Graham, remember how he consoled everyone who failed? From presidents to priests? Mr. Graham never condemned! He went the extra mile to console. A true intelligent gentleman, spiritual leader, friend, husband and father. A true American hero, a example of grace to humanity.

180

THE FUTURE IS OURS

Not money, but intelligence in the entire human race will be our greatest asset on Earth and beyond. That's what I believe and I know. That's what we take with us when we die. That's what we bring with us when we are born into this world.

Convinced, I am, of one thing: If we start to point fingers at the not so wealthy individuals and call them morally and spiritually bankrupt, then even poor nations, countries, continents, planets, fit in that category. Are the 90% of people on the planet all morally and spiritually bankrupt? ... just because they do not have money? Why are they poor? Why are countries poor? How about continents? I believe that our history is the mirror of our school of destiny.

As far as I know, the planet is wealthy, and so are its occupants. People are wealthy in God, that special force that drives them towards trust and discoveries,

181

With former Premier of Ontario Mike Harris during a national conference in Toronto.

Right, Catherine Clark, daughter of Prime Minister Joe Clark. She is the TV host of "Beyond Politics," CPAC.
I photographed Catherine many times. She is so beautiful, perfect version of a Canadian princess.

towards the very future which will take care to eliminate pain and suffering, forever.

I cannot wait to be in that elegant future in which our wealth will me measured in the quality of our spirit. I know right now that I am wealthy, and so are all humans who believe in honour, kindness and intelligence, before materialism.

There are many public stars on Earth today who I deeply admire for their humble spirits, intelligence and stability. They do not say much, they just do it. To name a few: Jeff Bezos; Richard Bronson; Bill Gates; Her Majesty Queen Elizabeth II; President Clinton and Secretary of State Hilary Clinton; Prime Minister Stephen Harper; Chancellor Angela Merkel and my most favourite American lady, Dolly Parton. I admire her for her realism. Many years ago I purchased her book, *"Dolly."* I simply, loved it. I also read *"My Life,"* by Bill Clinton. So much fun. In 2008 I read *"The Audacity of Hope,"* by President Barack Obama. In fact I read everything about the people I admire. I'm curious.

Years ago, watching President Reagan and First Lady, Nancy, I would close my eyes and pray for similar love and finesse. Not long after President Reagan's funeral, I received exactly that. We are being heard if we trust in possibility.

"Oprah! Before you leave ... I love you along with all your history. About the Sarah incident? This is a perfect example of our differences, reaction to events. I trust that if you could, you would take back part of it. But, it is in print ... So, we'll have to let it slide in history. We all do mistakes in life, don't we?—but *Mother History* reserves forgiveness for all of us. I'm positive that God will look after Sarah's future. She is loved by all those who care and understand, by me, you, regardless of her minor imperfection."

Long ago, as a young child, I was so in love with communication that just listening to the radio made me emotional—so, I would practice in the mirror, creating my own shows. Through history, everyone who

184

ended up involved in communication started young with the practice in the mirror. What I believe is that those designed to develop into communicators of some sort, as children are a bit private and appear to be happily preoccupied with imaginary games in which they ask and answer.

In my childhood, we had quite a nice library there, and I would go, take the three books I was permitted, run to the park near by, read, enjoy the pictures, meditate—then go back and ask for permission to take the next three books. Miss Titiana Singeorzan, the librarian, would ask, "Tell Me! Did you read these ones already? So fast?"

"Yes," I would answer.

"I think that you just flipped the pages. Let me ask you a few questions to find out if you really read them."

She was shocked to realize that I knew

everything in those books and she would give me the next three books. After a while she did not permit me to go twice a day for books, but I never suffered of book shortages. Books were everywhere, in every home. As I grew, working as a baby sitter for my teachers and my doctors—oh, the books ...

My grandparents had a huge amount of books (left from their 10 children). Then, there was the Bible and the books of songs.

It did not matter that I was born to a powerful father. I was just a baby when my parents divorced. My mother left the famous City of Sibiu and moved close to her parents in a German community surrounded by forests and mountains, 15 km from the (Bram-made) popular City of Bistrita, central Transylvania. She took the only job she could find to be able to raise her two children. She worked for the mayor's office. She

THE FUTURE IS OURS

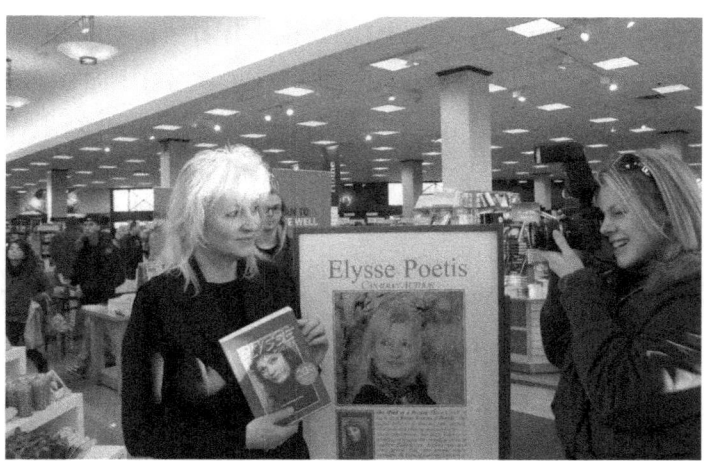

At Chapters Square One, Mississauga, posing for the young, beautiful SNAP Mississauga South reporter/photographer.

At Chapters Festival Hall, Toronto, posing with Dominic, the store manager—a truly intelligent young gentleman I admire.

also cleaned the school, the library, and the cinema hall. The keys from all those places/offices, including the library and the mayor's office, were hanging from a large metallic ring—and my mother had possession of all of them. If she went to clean the library, I was there reading and reading. If she cleaned the mayor's office, I was there in his chair reading everything on his desk. Wherever I turn, there were papers, books, newspapers, movies, telephone conversations, gossip, secrets, romances, mystique and drama. Pure theatrics everywhere.

One day I hypnotized the wasps at the post office's building. I was curious what was in that attic. We lived in that building for quite a few years, and no one dared to go in that attic because there were huge nests full of wasps. So, I talk to them. I told them that I just want to look there and they should not touch me.

188

THE FUTURE IS OURS

Wasps are like humans. They hear you and respect your wishes if the approach is sincere. Negotiations went fine, and I had deep trust that the wasps would not attack me. So, I made it to the attic, and as I turned the corner towards the other wing of the building I saw a little mountain covered in dust.

What could it be? I asked myself. Carefully, I approached, used my foot to move some things and I realized instantly that it was letters. A mountain of unopened letters under that blanket of dust.

Imagine my surprise and joy. Now I had my own library, safe from the rest of the world—and I had deadly wasps as security. Every day, in secrecy and unobserved, I would go there and take one envelope at a time, study it and its beautiful stamp, then open and read the content.

189

COVERED IN FLOWERS

I must have read hundreds of letters, when suddenly I detected an envelope out of this world. A royal stamp, a royal seal. After I blew the dust off, I did not have the heart to damage the envelope, so I kept it aside, safe. Days later, another one. Then another. By now, I would obsessively visit my discovery. I also started cutting off the ordinary envelopes stamps that I liked and hide them in a box. But my secrecy fell apart when my mother spied on me one day after she observed that I disappear somewhere, all alone. She followed me and when she realized that I went in the wasp infested attic, she nearly died of emotion.

"Elysse, come back. Come to Mama."

As I appear from above in front of her, with wasps zooming all around, ignoring me, I looked down at my mother and told her that I'm fine.

"What are you doing there?' She asked.

THE FUTURE IS OURS

"I'm reading!"

"Reading what?"

"Letters."

"What letters?"

"From the pile here."

"What pile?"

"A big pile of letters covered in dust."

"How many letters are in that pile?"

"Many ... Maybe thousands ..."

"Are those letters open?"

"Only the ones I opened."

"You didn't ... How many did you open?"

"Not that many, maybe hundreds ..."

"Elysse, bring some letters here and come down immediately. I have to see them."

Scared to abandon my special letters, I took them down with me. When my mother looked at the envelopes she said,

COVERED IN FLOWERS

"Oh, my God! These are royal envelopes. I'll take them to Mr. Schmidt," (the mayor).

It turned out that as all German men went to war, someone, probably even a woman (who must have died since), during the war placed all correspondence in that corner of the attic, for safety. So these historic letters, some secret/military letters, were there for over twenty years, and no one knew about them until me, a curious eight year old child, discovered them. Mr. Schmidt was very excited about the discovery. He went at night with a few intelligent, trusting German men and took the treasure away. I was asked to keep it secret—of course, until now, 48 years later.

Growing up between Germans made me like them. To this day, that order embedded in me, comes in very handy. That's why I'm productive. Books are many in our house. Happiness overwhelms me when I see my tiny grandchildren reaching for books. We all read them stories and they never have enough. They sing and talk to themselves all day long. My daughter's books from when she was a kid, I still have them in a transparent plastic box. Her children love that box.

In terms of my reading in the last 29 years here in Canada, you'll be surprised. Science, anything portraying the future, success stories. The more I read, the more I realize the infinite mountain in front of me. The lessons are infinite and so are we. Even our thoughts are being recorded in the cosmic libraries.

Right now, here beside me, the *Waterloo Region RECORD* is displaying '*Majesty in motion.*' **Queen Elizabeth II** scanning with her royal eyes a personalized *Black Berry* she received as a gift. With her elegant pastel hat, white gloves, her famous purse, double pearls and a RIM white coat match-

COVERED IN FLOWERS

ing RIM CEO Mike Lazaridis'—she toured the famous local giant *Research In Motion* yesterday, Monday July 5, 2010.

It all took place here around the corner from me, yet I could not go and be part of the crowd because I had my two adorable grandchildren here and it was too hot outside for little kids. This missed opportunity does not put a dent in my strong hope that one day I'll see the queen. I love the queen and I embedded her all over in my opera. Same with **The Queen Mother**, I even went and signed in The City of Brampton Special Book for her 100 th birthday.

I am a poet! Royalty beautifies my mind!

Royalty derives from creativity,
from poetry.

The End

THE FUTURE IS OURS

At right, I was four years old. Here after a crying episode at a photo studio in the city of Bistrita. My sister confused the photographer for a doctor. When she cried—I cried.

Below, enjoying my late teens in the city of Arad. Nature was always my favourite panoramic display, perfect artistic background.

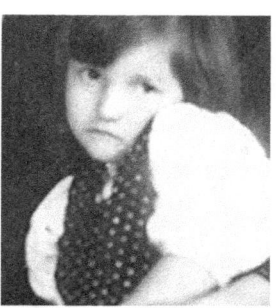

195

I HAVE A QUEEN
QUEEN ELIZABETH THE II,
QUEEN OF CANADA

A royal child, the child of King George VI and
Queen Elizabeth,
Sister of an attractive cosmic princess,
Princess Margaret ...

Glamorous bride of an elegant, generous
prince, Prince Philip, whose honourable desire to
protect her is forever unshakable ...

Mother of four beautiful children who quickly
arrived from the four cardinal points, equipped
with prestige ...
Ready to intrigue ...

Recipient of precious, wonderful grandchildren
The joy of her life, the charming youthful royal
future ...

I have a Queen!
A Queen who loves the planet,

THE FUTURE IS OURS

The Queen of Commonwealth,
With friends all over the world!

A Queen who loves people,
Heroes, wild flowers, smart dogs, brave horses,
A Queen who believes in GOD!

A Queen who prays for peace and tranquility
for the entire human race ...

A Queen who is admired, and loved ...
A Queen who rules in honour.

I am Canadian and I have a Queen!

A brilliant cosmic spirit, a noble I trust.

An extraordinary global model,
A model of royal honour and love ...
Love for beauty ... Love for peace ...
Love for life ... Love for all people ...

Your Majesty ... I Love You ... poetically Yours, ELYSSE

COVERED IN FLOWERS

My elegant readers, please stay positively engaged—let our infinite imagination be the invisible reality. From my corner on Earth, *The Technology Triangle of Canada,* I'll continue to monitor the beauty and the possibility out there. Excitement is what is awaiting for us, prosperity, peace, love and eternal life.

> "I am with you in harmony,
> I understand the hierarchy,
> The change of guard."

Oprah,
My dear entertainer,
I wish you cosmic love and life …
I wish you peace.

Elysse

— F I N A L E —

ELYSSE

POETIS

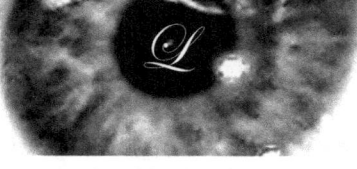

BIBLIOGRAPHY:

FERTILITY GODDESS SOVATA—*INSPIRATIONAL*

FOREVER LOVED—*THE LIFE AND DEATH OF LELU THE MANX*

I LOVE YOU—*CANADIAN POETRY*

OPRAH! BEFORE YOU LEAVE ... —*NOVEL/SATIRE*

THE BEAUTY OF NATURE—*PHOTOGRAPHY/NATURE*

THE HUNTER OF BEAUTY—*PHOTOGRAPHY/CANADA*

THE MIND OF A POETESS—*MEMOIR, TRUE STORY*

GREAT GLOBAL FUN IN CANADA & USA—*SOON TO COME*

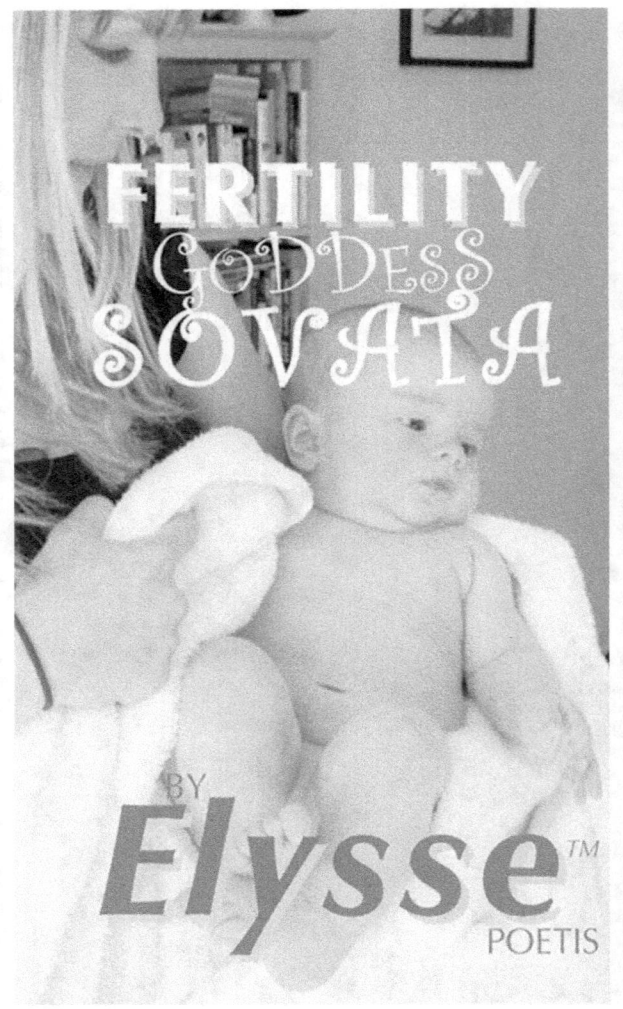

FERTILITY
GODDESS
SOVATA

BY
Elysse™
POETIS

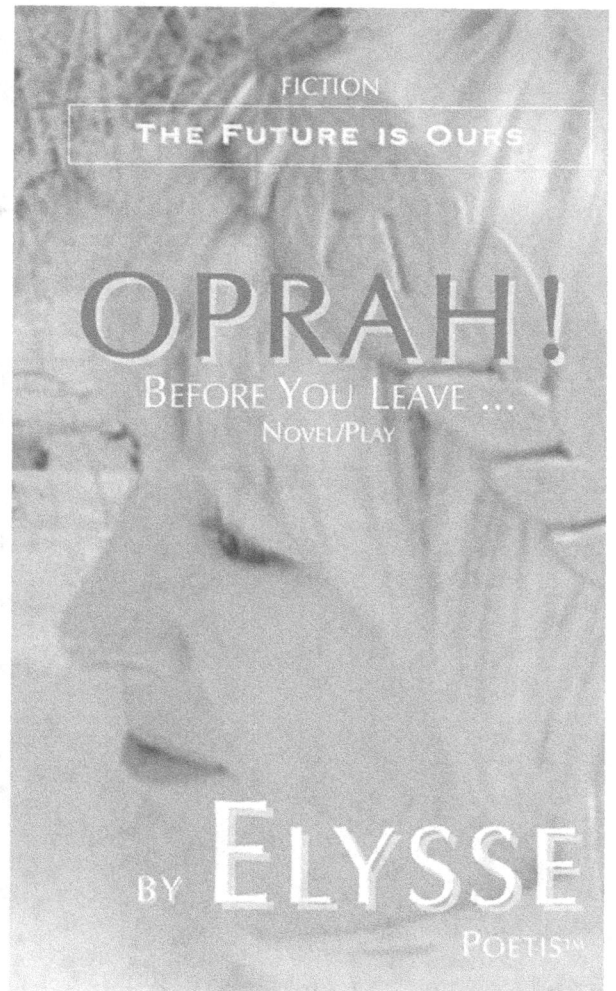

FICTION

THE FUTURE IS OURS

OPRAH!

BEFORE YOU LEAVE ...
NOVEL/PLAY

BY ELYSSE

POETIS™

206

ABOUT THE AUTHOR

Elysse was born on August 8, 1953, in the famous city of Sibiu, (Hermannstadt), Romania. Sibiu was known as *The City of Literature*. In 1997 was voted by the European Union *"The Capital of European Culture."*

Elysse left from behind the *iron curtains* at age 26 during the *cold war*. She experienced life in West Germany and later in a UN refugee camp near Vienna, Austria, from where in 1981 she was rescued by Canada. In her 29 years of Canadian life Elysse concentrated on communications.

The Award Winning Canadian author dedicated her books to humanity. Her artistic and literary work encompasses great dramatic and satiric stories, poetry and photography—variety fit for all ages. Elysse's artistic courtesy incorporates global taste. She resides with her husband/publisher in the Region of Waterloo, Ontario, Canada. www.elyssepoetis.com

www.ingramcontent.com/pod-product-compliance
Lightning Source LLC
Chambersburg PA
CBHW051827020726
47502CB00005B/1666